Tbe Mick

A Novel by
Patrick James Brown

This is a work of fiction. That means I made it up. Well, except for three major events: The Irish Easter Rebellion, World War I, and the burning of North Dakota's Capitol. Oh, and a reference to Al Capone, who is in no position to protest. Any other resemblance to any person, living or dead is merely an eerie coincidence.

Library of Congress Cataloging-in-Publication Data

Brown, Patrick James.

The Mick: a novel/by Patrick James Brown. — First Edition

ISBN 978-0-9963068-0-5 (softcover)

PRINTED IN THE UNITED STATES OF AMERICA

First Edition: November 2015

For Susan, the first true love of my life.

ACKNOWLEDGEMENTS

Although this is work of fiction, it is based on one central fact: North Dakota's first capital building burned down on December 28, 1930. As an adolescent I spent many hours in the old State Museum, fascinated by North Dakota's rich, but short, history. So I must first thank the many folks who put together all the displays. Perusing them filled many rainy days.

The Mick would be a much poorer work had it not been for the invaluable suggestions and superb edits by my good friend, Greg Lauser, who started out as my Sigma Chi Fraternity brother in 1968 and became my lifelong friend. Thanks, also, to my friend Katherine Tweed for her suggestions and her justifiable loathing of Jake Tilden.

Thanks, too, to my daughters, Kirsten, Sara, and Lindsay, for their love and encouragement during my struggle to write well.

It is also with the greatest amount of gratitude that I thank my teachers, most especially my high school English teachers, Maureen Beck, Sr. Angela, Sr. Barbara Ann, and Sr. Hugo, who recognized some talent in me, even though I did not, and Janet Line, my speech and drama instructor, who believed in me. In addition, I would be remiss if I did not thank my college professors at the University of North Dakota and Iowa State University, who worked hard to help me become a better writer.

Finally, I will just state the obvious: For what talent I have, I thank God, even though the Devil made me write parts of this book.

THE MICK

A Novel by
Patrick James Brown

PROLOGUE

The old bull blinked his good eye to relieve the itch and block out the driving snow. He swayed slightly from side to side to ease the pain in his 26 year-old knees.

The lone burr oak next to him stuck out like a blackened skeleton. It and the bull stood on the only small rise on the desolate wind-swept prairie. Both the tree and the bull braced against the frigid air that swept down from Canada. Blowing, evaporating, carving the snow drifts that turned the prairie into a frozen wasteland.

Here and there tufts of grass peeked through the crusts. Seeing them, instinct told the old bull that food was beneath the snow. All he had to do was rut his snout and eat. Even the act of exposing his food was painful. His neck and shoulder bones were thinning, grinding with each sweep of his massive head. He didn't know why, but the pain was greater than his need to feed. And so, two days ago, he had quit eating.

Now his body was consuming itself. The fat disappearing as his life slipped away, starving where he stood.

His had been a good life as a young bull in a herd of thousands. Then, because of his size, he had coaxed several cows with his and their calves to separate from the main herd and head north, close to their plush summer pastures in Canada. His small harem grew with each calving season. So did his size and power.

But the hunters found them. They had come with their wagons, and their fires, and their long rifles that ended his peaceful life.

He ran. Over one hill, through a small draw, up over another hill, and another and another, until he was too far away for the wagons and the smelly creatures with their skinning knives to chase.

He had wandered then. For years. Alone, he had become crafty. He knew that slivers of smoke meant the dangerous ones were near, and he avoided them when the new grass grew tall, when it turned brown, and when cold whiteness covered it making life harder to bear.

He would have been lonely if he had known what loneliness was. He only sensed that his urge to mount the cows had disappeared long ago. He didn't even want to be with a herd. All he had cared about was a full belly and enough water or snow to quench his thirst. But even those instincts had waned.

Two days ago, his hurting joints finally stole his will to live. He was tired, freezing.

First he felt the sharp pain in his ribs. It tore through his chest and ripped through his lungs. They were on fire. He fell to his knees and then he heard it.

The Sharps bullet always strikes before the report reaches the prey's ears.

-1-

ḃAON

Dublin, Ireland
Easter Thursday, 1916

Jack O'Connor shivered violently. His ratty coat, which hung on him like an empty potato sack, was soaked through by the relentless spring rain. It chilled his body. Fear chilled his soul.

He huddled close to his Da in the dark, wet alley, crouching to stay out of the light cast by an old gas light across the shadowy street that passed the alley.

Paddy O'Connor glanced about nervously. In Jack's sixteen years, he had never seen his father show any fear. But now his Da was afraid.

"Get ready, boy. And keep yer head down," he whispered.

Jack was tall for his age with long muscular legs that were starting to cramp. He moved ever so slightly. It was just enough for his foot to slip on wet cobblestones, lose his balance, and drop the old revolver he had been given.

Eamon O'Shea, the band's leader, turned to the noise, cuffed the boy on the head, picked up the revolver and thrust it at Paddy.

"Stupid farmers. Keep the lad in line, or I'll kill him myself," O'Shea hissed under his breath.

Paddy glared at O'Shea, then blinked and looked down at his son.

"He'll be fine, Eamon," he said. "And don't be hittin' my boy or threatening us. We're not the enemy."

Paddy handed the gun back to Jack.

"Hold on this time, boyo," he whispered. "We're all nervous. Just don't shoot yerself… or me."

Jack O'Connor held the gun stiffly, swallowed hard, and nodded.

Just then, they heard the sound of boots striking pavement. Many boots.

A column of thirty British police rounded the corner twenty yards away and marched down the deserted street toward the alley.

O'Shea whispered, barely audible, "Wait until they pass. Then we'll attack from behind."

The police marched closer, the sound of their boots echoing in the still night.

The Sinn Fein men crouched, waiting. One man nervously checked his revolver.

The police approached the front of the alley. In unison their boots stomped to a halt on the wet street.

"Left face," ordered a voice. "Present arms!"

Jack looked up at his father.

"Da …?"

Paddy O'Connor thrust his hand over the boy's mouth. "Shhhh!"

Across the street, opposite the alley opening, a man in dark clothing and wearing a knit cap pulled down low on his head watched the drama unfold. When the two columns of police faced the alley, he brought a brass whistle to his mouth. The shrilling shattered the night.

At the sound, O'Shea ducked under a nearby loading dock. One of the men, a short, thin shepherd with a club foot, charged clumsily out of the alley, screamed, and shot into the column of police.

"Feckin Brits. D-I-E."

The front row of police fired at the man, killing him instantly. The column behind them fired into the alley. The Irishmen wildly shot back, their lack of discipline apparent. One policeman fell. Gunfire and acrid smoke filled the night air. A bullet tore off Paddy O'Connor's face. Jack fired his pistol and crouched next to his father.

"DA, DA," he screamed, tears running down his cheeks.

Bullets zinged about him. He cradled the older man's head in his arms. Blood covered both of them. Jack wailed as more tears streamed down his face.

The police continued to fire, reload, fire, reload. Behind them, the dark figure in the doorway watched calmly. Then he stepped out of the doorway and walked slowly, fearlessly toward the policemen.

One of the other Irish revolutionaries, blood gushing from his chest, collapsed onto Jack, who was now covered in blood. Jack crawled out from under the man. He looked in front of himself and saw O'Shea cowering under the loading dock. Their eyes met. O'Connor threw his revolver at O'Shea, who caught it as he fired his own revolver at O'Connor, missing.

A police sergeant stopped firing his revolver at the men in the alley. He saw them all lying on the ground.

"Stop firing. STOP FIRING."

The other police stopped firing a few at a time. Moans of wounded and dying men punctuated the silence.

Crouching, Jack O'Connor ran along the building. In the darkness, the police didn't see him. Suddenly a light came on in a window. The light shined down on O'Connor.

He froze.

The sergeant saw O'Connor, raised his gun and quickly fired three shots. O'Connor turned his head toward the gunfire, and ducked. All three bullets struck the brick just above his head. Now scared into moving, he ran along the building.

Seeing O'Connor run, the sergeant grabbed a rifle from the nearest policeman, carefully aimed, and fired once.

O'Connor raced headlong to the corner of the nearest building. As he turned the corner, the rifle bullet ricocheted off a brick striking him in the side.

The sergeant threw the rifle back at the policeman.

"Well, go after him, Smythe," he hissed.

Smythe adjusted the rifle in his hands and with several others, cautiously approached the alley.

"Run after him, you idiots!"

In the alley, wounded men lay scattered about, moaning. The policemen, pointing their rifles ready to fire, hurried through the bodies on the ground.

Holding his left side, O'Connor ran along the dark side of the street, hugging the buildings. Finally, he turned a corner and ran right into the man in dark clothes who had anticipated O'Connor's escape route. The man grabbed O'Connor by the shoulders. In their struggle, O'Connor, covered in wet blood, slipped out of the man's arms and ran. About a half block away, O'Connor turned his head around.

The man calmly watched him go. He walked around the corner and continued toward the alley where the sergeant, his pistol at his side, was stepping through the bodies, shooting any that moved or made a sound in the head. Finally, he stopped to listen.

"You can come out now, O'Shea," he said.

O'Shea crawled from beneath the loading dock.

"You enjoyed that," O'Shea said.

"It's one of life's little pleasures. But then, they are only Irish. And poor starving farmers, at that. Less mouths for the Crown to feed."

At the end of the alley, the man appeared. The sergeant and O'Shea turned toward him.

"Everything went smoothly, captain," the sergeant reported.

"I watched."

He faced O'Shea. "You'd best go now."

As O'Shea turned to leave, the captain gave an almost imperceptible nod to the sergeant, who violently clubbed O'Shea on the back of the head with his pistol. O'Shea slumped to the ground.

"The Micks would drown him like a rat if it wasn't for us," the captain sneered. "Leave him. He can claim he got knocked down in the fray."

"I took care of the others," the sergeant said, smiling. "Are you wounded, sir?" he asked the officer as he spied blood on the captain's coat.

"No, I bumped into the lad, it's his blood. I let him run. He'll tell the other Sinn Feiners in the county that the ambush turned into a slaughter. They'll decide we're too powerful and give up. With any luck, they'll figure out one of their own turned traitor for a nice plot of land, and then we'll be free of O'Shea, too."

With his toe, the captain lifted the shoulder of one of the dead men and then dropped it.

Gazing down the dark street in the direction O'Connor ran, he sighed. "We will need to find that boy," he said to no one in particular.

Then, looking over the carnage, he and the sergeant walked down the alley to where the other policemen waited, gathered around two of their own who lay dead on the cobblestones.

~2~

Dó

Covered in dried blood, wet with dew, Jack O'Connor lay at the foot of a large oak, curled into the fetal position to try to stay warm. In spite of the chilled morning air, he was dead to the world.

A tall, stately middle-aged man dressed in woolen pants, a leather jacket, and carrying a custom-made Purdey double-barreled shotgun walked quietly toward O'Connor. His shiny black boots slid through the tall, wet grass. He stepped close to the sleeping boy and gently nudged him with the tip of the barrel. Getting no response, he gently kicked the boy on the sole of his right foot.

O'Connor woke with a start and moaned. Clearing his eyes, he stared up at the man's shotgun and crept toward the base of the tree.

"So, you are alive," said the man. "Up."

O'Connor tried to get up, but winced in pain. The man firmly grabbed O'Connor's arm and pulled him to his feet.

"Friends ... or enemies shoot you?"

"Neither, sir. I was running in the dark and some eejit left a pitchfork next to the road. I tripped and fell on it. Damn near run me through, it did."

"Looks like you have lost a great amount of blood," said the man. "'Tis a miracle you're still alive."

"True. True. But ya see, earlier I had been watching a

farmer slaughter a sheep, sir. And I got too close and, and I slipped and fell in the blood. And so I got it all over me. And that's when I started runnin' home, sir."

Recognizing a tall tale, the man looked skeptically at O'Connor.

"A sheep ya say? Seems a few sheep had a bit of a problem in Dublin night before last. I'm hoping your sheep had a bit more wool ... and brains."

O'Connor suddenly turned pale, bent over and vomited on the man's boots. The man looked down in disgust and wiped his boots off in the wet grass.

"Come, boyo. We had better plug up that fork hole in your belly."

"I must be getting home, sir. Me ma will be worried."

"Your ma would die of the fright if she saw you like this, boyo," said the man.

The man put the shotgun in his left hand and bent down. He put his right hand under O'Connor's left arm pit, pulled him up, and half carried O'Connor to his horse, which stood patiently on the path near the oak. The man slid his Purdey in a polished leather scabbard and, still holding O'Connor's coat collar with his left hand, grabbed the saddle's pommel with his right hand and mounted his horse. With little effort, he pulled O'Connor up by the collar of his coat and sat him on the horse's withers. That's when the metallic stench of the boy's blood hit him.

"Hold his mane tight, boyo."

The boy had passed out, so the man held the reins in one hand and the back of O'Connor's coat in the other. He gently nudged the horse's ribs and they trotted down the path into the rising sun.

Minutes later, horse and riders turned onto an approach

and passed through a massive stone gate over which was a stone arch with the words "Scotland, My Home Is Still Ye" carved in Scotch Gaelic.

The British had conscripted the man's ancestors and forced them to settle in the west coast of Ireland in hopes they would tame and help subjugate the wild Irish. Instead, these Presbyterian Scots assimilated with the Roman Catholic natives. Over the years, Scottish men married Irish women due to a shortage of their own kind. Some became Catholic, others, like the man, had stayed true to their race and Protestant religion.

At the ripe old age of 10, the man announced to his parents that he wanted to design grand buildings, and asked if they wouldn't please sell a sheep or two so he could attend university in England.

Six years later, his parents sold two hectares to a neighbor, and shipped the boy off to Eaton boarding school, where he excelled in every subject, then on to study art and architecture in Italy.

He loved Italy, more than he loved his beloved Ireland, and studied the massive churches and strolled in awe through Roman ruins, constantly marveling at what the Roman builders had accomplish with their primitive tools and scaffolds.

Upon returning to Ireland the day after he turned 26, full of knowledge and the arrogance of youth, he had sought positions with the top architectural firms in Belfast and, reluctantly, Dublin, to no avail. He finally settled in Limerick where he joined a small building company and made a reputation for designing beautiful and functional Irish cottages, which he grew to detest.

In his spare time, he dreamed of owning a grand estate

of his own, so he designed a magnificent country home, with horse barns and sheep shearing huts.

Once a month, he borrowed a friend's gelding and rode the six hours to his parents' home. Every time he approached it, he envisioned the buildings he designed there at the end of the road.

On the man's thirty-first birthday, a minister showed up at the builder's office asking for him. The man didn't recognize him. He would be hard pressed to recognize any minister.

"I'm here to see Clayton Andrews," he said reverently.

Andrews looked up from his drawing table.

"That's me."

"'Fraid I've come with bad news, then. Can we talk in private?"

Andrews led the man through a narrow hall out to a storage yard where the masons kept fresh cut stone.

"You may want to sit, Mr. Andrews."

"I'll stand."

Gently grasping Andrews' upper left arm, the minister soulfully looked him in the eye.

"Your ma and pa died in a most tragic fire," he began, "probably started in the main chimney during the night two nights ago. The house is lost. The funeral is tomorrow morning at 10. I've brought a carriage so you can ride back with me. We can talk about God's plan on the way."

"We'll no talk of God's plan, preacher," he said jerking his arm from the minister's hand. "I cannot believe burning my parents in their sleep is God's plan!"

Andrews stormed off around the building leaving the stunned minister standing amidst the stones. "I'll find me own way home," he yelled at the stunned Presbyterian.

Andrews nearly killed his friend's horse, pushing him relentlessly. He had cried, sobbed was more like it, half-way home when the reality of what had happened finally sunk in. Then he was furious, at his father for not hiring a chimney sweep, at his mother for not nagging her husband about hiring a damn chimney sweep, at the chimney sweep for not making a regular visit to clean the damn chimneys, at the minister for talking about God's plan in the same breath as he gave him the news, at God for being so cruel. And then he sobbed louder.

The funeral was a dreary affair at his parents' farm, even though the sun shone brightly on the dew-covered fields. Andrews insisted that, contrary to the demands of the minister that they be buried in the church cemetery, his parents would be buried at the top of a hill overlooking the farmyard.

Two days later, Clayton Andrews began designing his own estate, which he would build atop his parent's burned out house.

Two years later, Andrews had saved enough money, so that combined with the sale of all his livestock, a generous bank loan, and a great deal of guilt, he had built the grandest estate in the county.

It was a show piece, from large columns and a massive winding staircase. British and Scotch-Irish land owners throughout Ireland consigned him to design and build large country homes, which they financed by raising the rent on their poor Irish tenant farmers.

Clayton Andrews became rich and one of Ireland's most eligible bachelors, sought after by the parents of young, beautiful and not so beautiful daughters.

At a barn dance his neighbor held in his honor, Andrews

spied a young woman who wore a Tartan dress of some clan he didn't recognize. She had auburn hair, a freckled angular face with high cheek bones, and a shapely body. She seemed to sense his stare. She looked him square in the eyes until, completely overcome by her beauty, he averted his eyes.

Her name was Colleen, he found out from the party's host. She was eligible, so he began the courtship process by calling on her at her parents' home.

Years later, she would tell their only child, a daughter they had named Brigid, that theirs was love at first sight, although she made Clayton follow all the local customs before she accepted his proposal.

The Andrews had an almost idyllic life. Barn dances. Lavish dinners. Fine furniture. Colleen took care of the house and Brigid. Clayton managed the land and continued to design large homes and commercial buildings.

Neither of them, however, could manage Brigid, who was nearly the spitting image of her mother, from the freckles and high cheekbones, to her athletic body, with one exception. While her mother had auburn hair, Brigid's hair was flaming red.

Once Brigid learned to walk, she ran. When she learned to ride a horse, she rode too fast. At the county fair, she raced her horse against horses jockeyed by boys much older than her, and beat them handily through reckless riding. She had even demanded to wrestle the village boys, and threw a tantrum when her mother wouldn't permit such disgraceful behavior. She was, in no uncertain terms, the spoiled only child of well-to-do parents.

Brigid galloped her horse to the house from a field to the west as Clayton rode up carrying the boy. She reined in her horse and jumped off.

"Father!" she yelled.

"I told you not to scare the sheep," he admonished her.

Ignoring him as she usually did, she asked, "What have ye got there?"

"A lad who needs our help. Now get yer ma."

Clayton and Colleen carried Jack O'Connor into the house.

Three weeks later, O'Connor, clean and dressed in other clothes and carrying a small bag, walked down the drive leading from the estate to the road. Standing on the large home's porch, Clayton and Colleen watched him. Brigid stood at the window of her second story bedroom, peeking out between lace curtains.

She remembered his days in the bedroom next to hers, how he had almost died. O'Connor's life had hung on the verge of death for close to eight days.

Her father had summoned a surgeon from Limerick to tend to the boy's wounds. When the doctor saw how pale the boy was, he told Andrews the boy would probably die from blood loss, but he would treat his wounds and they could hope for the best.

"He's lucky," the doctor had said. "The bullet didn't go very far into him, but it still caused a lot of bleeding. How did he get shot? There was an attempted uprising in Dublin Easter Week. Was he there? I don't want to know."

Getting the bullet out had proven difficult. Because it had ricocheted off a brick wall, the bullet had not been round when it struck O'Connor. And when the doctor had stuck his finger in the hole to find the bullet, he had punctured his finger on the bullet's sharp edge.

Unable to use a surgical instrument for fear of tearing more tissue, the surgeon improvised. He had to use something that would grab the bullet and protect the boy's innards from the sharp edges.

"Clayton, bring me a small-caliber bullet mould," he finally requested. By inserting the closed bullet mould into the boy's wound, the doctor had then been able to open it up, enclose the ragged bullet in the mould, and extract it.

"You are a genius, Eamon," Clayton Andrews said.

"And yet," he replied holding up the bullet, "I am still your friend."

The doctor cleaned the bullet hole with alcohol, which brought moans of pain from the boy, so he forced the boy to drink sips of laudanum to ease the pain as he stitched the hole with a long curved needle and black waxed sail thread.

"They're looking for a survivor, Clayton," the doctor said. "It's all over the papers."

"I can read," Andrews responded.

"We don't want either of us to get in trouble, so keep him in the house for at least a month until things quiet down."

"Good advice," Andrews intoned, "and I know how you like to gossip, so don't!"

As the Andrews watched the doctor ride off, Clayton Andrews faced his wife and daughter.

"Not a word about any of this to anyone, ya hear?"

"We understand, father," his wife said.

O'Connor had only taken small sips of whatever fluid they had put to his thin, pale lips. Finally, thanks to his stubbornness and their round-the-clock care, he had begun to gain strength.

Brigid had been curious about how the boy came to be shot, or, as he insisted, stabbed with a pitchfork. When he could finally sit up and talk, she had pestered him until he admitted the truth. But she wanted to know everything about his life, wouldn't let him pretend to doze off.

Reluctantly, and in bits, he told her the story of his life.

"Me pa is dead. Died in the fight I told you about. He and ma are … were … farmers, but now I don't know how ma's going to pay the rent that our landlord just raised … again."

O'Connor choked.

"Pa even had a hard time coming up with the payments … We was always hungry. I can't ever remember not being hungry. Sometimes, when we didn't have oats or potatoes, we had to eat bugs and boiled grass. Even ate worms."

Brigid had gasped at this and run out of the room. O'Connor fell asleep. After she had washed the vomit from her mouth, Brigid came back into the bedroom and sat on the side of the bed. She wiggled the boy's feet until he woke up. She gave him water in the glass on the bedside table.

"Tell me more," she pleaded.

He gulped the water, cleared his throat.

"I was always hungry," he started.

"You already said that," Brigid reminded him.

He looked at her quizzically.

"I did?"

"Yes, ya eejit."

"Then where'd I leave off?"

"At the worms."

"Oh … Um … Our clothes was always tattered. Ma did her best, but thread was hard to come by, so she'd unravel part of an old flour sack for the thread and then use a piece of that sack to patch up a hole in me or my brother or sister's clothes. We looked like walking sacks," he laughed.

"Go on," she said. "What did you do for fun?"

"Pa made a ball out of straw and the skin of a dog that

died. We kicked that up and down the road and in our yard until it fell apart. That was fun. Not much else was."

"You didn't even have a proper ball," Brigid asked, stunned.

"Whatcha mean! That was a proper ball!"

"Pa and ma never had much fun. Once in a while, at night, we'd hear them laugh a little, but not much.

"Pa would leave the house most nights after dark and walk up the road to a neighbor's place. Ma said he was at meetings to try to get the landlord to lower the rent and for the Brits to stop arresting our friends for not doing nothing and to get the bloody hell out of Ireland and leave us alone forever," O'Connor said and raised his head up from the pillows, his face red with anger.

This scared Brigid, but she put both hands on the boy's shoulders and gently pushed him back.

She eased herself off the side of the bed and quietly rushed out of the room stunned at what she had heard, believing not one word of it.

Now, the boy was leaving, walking out of their lives.

"I can't stay," the boy said two days earlier at breakfast between mouthfuls of thick bacon, soda bread, and oatmeal.

"Slow down, boyo. You'll no doubt eat again." The man laughed.

"Nothing this good, sir, no doubt."

When the boy could finally get out of bed, the man had taken him for short walks around the estate. Game paths wove through the woods that surrounded the tilled fields, and they hiked the paths, ducking under low-hanging branches, climbing over fallen trees. The activity had helped restore O'Connor's agility and muscle tone.

The jagged hole in his side had become a two-inch

wound, held together by stitches put there by someone, O'Connor didn't know whom. The woman told him he could pull them out when the wound could stay together on its own.

Some twenty days after the bullet had come out of him, Colleen Andrews watched the lanky 14-year-old walk out of their lives.

"Poor lad. Such a pity."

"The real pity, Colleen, is that he is already a liar and a hooligan. We just postponed his dying."

"Clayton," she scolded. "He's just a boy. Did he ever thank you?"

"He did not say much at all."

As O'Connor stepped onto the road at the end of their drive, Clayton and Colleen Andrews, descendants of Scottish Protestant transplants, walked back into their home.

"The Brits'll be looking for him," he said. "Remind the staff that no boy was ever here. I'll horsewhip anyone who says otherwise."

-3-

TRÍ

Jack O'Connor walked all day and half the night before he crawled into a hay stack and fell asleep. Hungry and still tired, he finally reached home at dusk on the third day.

It was eerily quiet as O'Connor slowly approached the house. The front door was slightly open. He pushed it and stuck his head in the narrow opening.

The smell made him gag. He staggered back and vomited bile. When his nausea subsided, O'Connor stood, went back to the door and pushed it all the way open. Inside, children's bodies were strewn about. Holding his nose, O'Connor cautiously walked through the doorway.

Seven children, an infant boy, two toddler boys and three slightly older girls, and an adolescent girl, lay bloated on the floor. O'Connor scanned the room. In the far corner, his mother sat on the floor, slowly rocking from side to side. Her scalp and forehead were encrusted with dried blood, her nose broken. She had a vacuous stare on her face.

"Ma!"

The woman rocked the bundle in her arms.

"Oh, Ma. No!"

Ignoring the smell of death, O'Connor slowly walked to his mother and slumped down on the floor next to her.

"Ma! What ... MA?"

She slowly turned her head to him.

"They came for you, Jack. 'Where's the boy,' they says.

'All we want is the Sinn Feiner!' I told them I didn't know any Sinn Feiner. All hooligans, I say."

O'Connor started to sob.

His mother looked down at the baby.

"Hush now, Megan. Don't cry."

O'Connor gently took his mother's chin in his hand and turned her to face him.

"Ma?"

"They said they'd take my babes. Like drowning pups, they said. I remember screaming."

"Hush, now," she sobbed, looking down again at the bundle in her arms.

"Who did, Ma? Who did this?" he asked her as he gripped her shoulders.

"Police, they were. One ... awful. You've got to go, now. You're my only baby left."

She looked back down at the dead newborn in her arms. O'Connor saw that his baby sister's skull was crushed.

"Go! They'll come back when they don't find you. Promise me you'll go."

"I promise, Ma."

Still looking down, she began to sing.

"Tura lura, lura ... hush now, don't you cry ...", she whispered with her final breaths.

Her head dropped and her chin hit her bony chest. O'Connor shook her shoulders. "Jasus, Ma."

He collapsed, the exertions of the past three days after being bedridden for the better part of three weeks and the tragedy of this awful homecoming taking their toll.

O'Connor didn't know how long he slept, but awoke to the nightmare he had confronted in twilight. As the eastern sky began its early morning glow, he buried his younger siblings in separate tiny graves.

As he dug the graves in the rocky soil behind the house, he tried to recall something about each child, the boys he taught to kick the ball and herd the sheep, the girls he tickled and threw into the air to make them giggle. His grief overwhelmed his memories, but he fought to push through at least one or two for the older ones.

Finally, O'Connor knelt next to the largest mound of dirt. He smoothed it one last time with blistered hands. Then he grabbed one more pile of grass and piled it on the mound hoping to conceal it. When finished to his satisfaction, he fell down on it. Other mounds were close by.

"Good bye, Ma. Someday, I'll even the score."

-4-

ceatbair

Twenty Miles South of Manthois, France
November, 1918

All around him soldiers screamed as German shells tore their limbs from them. Bodies flew through the air some yards in front of him. Through the heavy fog, Jack O'Connor could hear the sporadic bark of machine guns.

His uniform was caked in mud, some fresh, most of it days old and stiff. From where he was standing in the hastily dug trench, he could see the small phosphorous fires and dead Austrian soldiers that littered the battlefield. The memory of finding his poor dead brothers and sisters flashed through the fog of battle.

Just as the whistle grew louder, a hand pulled O'Connor into the mud.

"Get down, you stupid Mick!"

Two nights later, after the British and New Zealand divisions had advanced three hundred yards, O'Connor had sneaked behind the enemy lines. He wore a black sweater, blackened his face and hands with boot black, and crouch-crawled under barbed wire that marked the Austrian perimeter. He had undertaken dangerous clandestine missions many times since landing in Calais on the French coast thirteen months earlier, and they had become routine – sharpen knife, don black clothes, pray, blacked face and hands, report to sergeant, leave camp, crawl under a hundred meters of razor-sharp barbed wire, kill … the same almost every night and every night the same memories flooded his consciousness fighting for attention.

After spending eight months living in his family cottage and doing odd jobs for neighbors to earn a meal or two each day, he had tired of sneaking around to avoid the Brit police during their unannounced visits to his village. When he heard about the big war and that the Brits would give him a uniform and a decent meal, he had lied about his age to enlist in their army.

It had been easy because the army needed bodies and his was just what they needed. At six-feet-two-inches, with a swarthy complexion, and without a birth certificate to prove otherwise, the seventeen year-old just got stamped through by the frazzled volunteer at the enlistment bureau.

During basic training O'Connor quickly proved himself ready to fight better than most of his fellow enlistees. He ran faster, handled weapons better, and excelled at bayonet training and hand-to-hand combat training. After the first two weeks, during which he suffered constant disparaging comments about his brogue and his nationality, these demonstrations of his skills at fighting and killing earned him the respect of his mates and the snide comments all but disappeared. One day, a month into his group's training, three raw recruits from the slums of Liverpool harassed him in the mess hall. Two of his platoon members jumped up from the table to shut the men up before any damage was done, but when the three new recruits persisted in deriding the Mick, his platoon members stepped aside, shrugged their shoulders, and smiled at O'Connor, who dispatched the Liverpudlians before his platoon's drill sergeant strode over to quell the disturbance.

"Nice work, O'Connor," he said looking at the three men laying on the mess hall floor. "Finish eating and meet me on the parade grounds. Oh, and bring your platoon mates along."

Five minutes later, O'Connor and his platoon gathered around their drill sergeant, who threw a training rifle at O'Connor.

"Hold it over your head until I tell you to put it down, Mr. O'Connor," he growled. "Now men," he addressed the rest of the platoon and pointed at O'Connor, "this is what happens when you damage the King's property, even if that property are three arses."

Then, without looking at O'Connor, he commanded, "All right, Mr. O'Connor, you've proved my point. Lower the weapon and return to your barracks."

Other platoon members laughed and they all joked with O'Connor about the incident as they walked to their barracks.

Once his group landed in France, O'Connor volunteered to scout ahead of the army and report the enemy's location. Occasionally, just because he could and because he loved the feeling it gave him, he would sneak across "No Man's Land" with its sharp barbed wire, treacherous bomb holes, and bodies rotting in abandoned trenches, into a Kraut camp and quietly slit a few throats.

This night was no different. He had been through it dozens of times. Barely visible in the dark, moonless night, he stood behind the scarred remnants of an old oak tree. In his left hand he held his favorite weapon – a large razor-sharp knife, as black and evil as the gates of Hell.

A lone Austrian soldier, stupidly wearing a gas mask

and holding his rifle in front of him like a pitch fork, bayonet affixed, approached O'Connor's position. As the soldier got closer, O'Connor inched around the opposite side of the tree trunk.

The Austrian soldier's hair on the back of his neck stood up. He stopped, stiffened his body, listened, and looked from side to side. Hearing nothing, he relaxed his stance, reached up and pulled off his gas mask.

O'Connor saw his face, barely visible in the blackness of night. He had what appeared to be the baby-faced complexion and peach fuzz of an Aryan, and was either 17 or 18, O'Connor couldn't tell which. Whatever age, he looked a lot like a Brit policeman to O'Connor.

The Austrian leaned his rifle on his thigh, reached into a pocket and pulled out a pipe and tobacco. He began to tamp tobacco in the pipe when he heard a soft scrape of fabric on tree bark behind him. O'Connor shot his right hand over the young soldier's mouth. Fear crossed the boy's face and his pale blue eyes grew large. O'Connor leaned around so the boy could see him and shook his head back and forth slightly.

"Sshhh," he whispered kindly.

The boy nodded his understanding. O'Connor relaxed his hand and removed it from the boy's mouth.

O'Connor stepped all the way around and took a half step back. He stared into the boy's eyes. The boy's uniform, boots, and hands were caked in mud; his baby face was smudged soot black, his eyes hollow. He stared back at O'Connor for three seconds, then his eyes narrowed and he slightly moved his head. As the boy-soldier grabbed for the barrel of his rifle, O'Connor calmly slashed his throat, and with his other hand, stifled the boy's cries.

Then O'Connor crouch-ran his way through the camp

throughout the night, methodically, silently slitting the throats of four other unlucky Austrian soldiers. One of them had seen O'Connor at the last second and grabbed the razor-edged blade of O'Connor's knife, severing all the fingers on his right hand when O'Connor pulled away the blade. O'Connor silenced his guttural scream with a quick slash across his throat. As dawn approached, O'Connor snuck back to British lines. At least that's where he thought he was going.

He was lost and confused. O'Connor had been trained to visually mark his way and not be followed. But something was wrong. The tree branch patterns he had committed to memory were gone, obliterated during the night by shells from British cannons. Constant drizzle had wiped out any tracks he might have left earlier.

He had hunkered down behind a large stump and waited for the sun to peek over the Austrian encampment. He heard distant angry shouts from soldiers as they discovered the bodies of the men he had killed.

When the sun finally cast enough light over the eastern horizon, O'Connor headed in the opposite direction. He wove his way, back-tracked, sloshed in rivulets of water that meandered down small valleys until finally, with the sun at mid-morning, O'Connor approached the shallow trenches.

He stopped and listened with trained ears – no noise, no clatter of canteens, no motor sounds, no sentry challenging him.

In battle, any well-conceived plan can turn to chaos once bullets fly and men scream. Even when there is order among disciplined soldiers, often the only communication is orders quietly spread from soldier to soldier—except when a soldier is unable to hear them.

While O'Connor was off creating chaos behind enemy

lines, his company had been ordered to advance to the northwest to try and outflank the Austrians.

He would follow their tracks, he decided. O'Connor easily found the ruts of the horse-drawn cannons, the mud mush caused by a hundred boots, the outlying horseshoe prints of the officers' mounts.

O'Connor estimated they had pulled out a couple of hours before he entered the Austrians' camp. His company had a six-hour head start, but O'Connor was tired and in no hurry. Besides, he needed a cup of tea and some food. He looked around to make sure he hadn't been followed and then he headed in the general direction of his company.

Hours later, hungrier and ornerier, O'Connor was trudging on the narrow grassy shoulder along the side of a muddy road when he heard the sputtering motor before a motorcycle with sidecar appeared over the hill in front of him.

O'Connor cursed and slid into the ditch, but the rider saw him and waved. O'Connor stood, feet apart, and raised his rifle. The motorcycle slid to a stop in the mud.

"I surrender, sport," shouted the rider, a British soldier wearing goggles and a leather helmet. "You lost?"

"Tryin' to find me unit, that's all."

"What unit's that, Mick?"

"Twelfth Infantry."

"Look in my side mirror, corporal. You're the only sorry S-O-B left. They pulled out last night. Hop in, I'll take you in."

O'Connor crawled into the side-car. The rider rocked the clutch forward with his muddy left foot, cranked back the throttle with his gloved right hand. The Harley-Davidson FUS lurched forward just as the impact of the other soldier's words hit O'Connor.

Stunned by the thought of being abandoned, he gazed over the pock-marked fields, shattered trees, and tank tracks that scarred the countryside seeing nothing, yet the images of war burning into his subconscious.

He had no idea how long they rode or how long ago he had fallen asleep despite the jostling when the operator roughly shook his right shoulder. O'Connor awoke with a start and grabbed for his knife, but reality set in when the motorcycle slid to a stop at a muddy intersection.

"I'm headin' to the front, mate," the soldier yelled above the Harley's rumble. "Delivering maps to the general. You'll be wanting to head down that road a few kilometers to the rear," he yelled louder. "Might even get yerself a hot meal."

Sore in places he didn't know he had, O'Connor forced himself out of the sidecar and stood in front of the bike.

"Why did they retreat?" he yelled.

The man shut off the motorcycle. "They didn't. Just repositioned. We found out the Gerry's planned a sneak attack. Your colonel didn't want to lose troops in a nighttime battle, so he pulled out well ahead of the attack. Where were you?"

"Busy," O'Connor replied.

As O'Connor trudged through the mud, he heard the motorcycle sputter twice and then rumble off in the opposite direction.

O'Connor finally came to a spot in the road where the grassy shoulder gave him a path out of the mud. The going was easier and faster, so he made good time, but he was exhausted and running out of energy. Even the toughest warriors need food and water. And sleep, merciful sleep.

Just as he was about to let himself collapse on a grassy knoll at the top of a short rise, he spied a truck on the road below his position. He trudged on another hundred meters and stumbled up to the rear of the truck. Someone grabbed him under his arms and he was lifted into the truck. Once inside, he half sat, half laid on the truck bed and felt the mouth of a canteen at his cracked lips. He drank voraciously and passed out.

When he woke up, he was alone in the back of a Red Cross truck as it bumped along and slid side to side through the ruts in the muddy road that ran past hospital tents. A light snow fell on the string of crippled and bandaged soldiers limping beside the road.

The truck slid to a stop. Stiff from sitting in the cold, O'Connor stumbled out of the back and wended his way through the column of wounded soldiers and the hospital tents to the mess tent.

"You look like shite," the mess cook said as he dished some steaming gray slop onto the hard biscuits in O'Connor's bowl.

"So does this," O'Connor said.

"Ah, but it's hot shite," the cook laughed.

Despite its appearance, the hot food tasted good, and O'Connor ate like it was his first hot meal in years when it had only been several weeks.

He was on his second helping when a young British officer approached and stood beside O'Connor.

"You were with the Twelfth Infantry," he said more as a statement than a question.

"I am," responded O'Connor.

"Then why aren't you with them, Mick?"

"I was busy when they pulled out."

"Busy deserting?"

"No, Sir," O'Connor said with a sneer. "Just busy doing

your dirty work."

"I won't countenance insolence, especially from a Mick," the young officer snapped.

Other soldiers in the mess tent now looked up at the pair. One of them slid out the rear tent flap. O'Connor continued to eat.

"Stand at attention when I talk to you, soldier," he yelled as he slapped his riding crop on the table next to O'Connor's bowl.

Just as O'Connor reached for his knife, another officer approached.

"A word, lieutenant," he said curtly to the younger officer.

The two officers walked between rows of tables filled with war weary soldiers and out the front of the tent.

"I'm sorry, Mr. O'Connor," said the captain when he returned alone. "The lieutenant didn't know your special role in our little war. You've done enough, so why don't we just get you out of here and on your way home," he said, then turned to leave. He turned back to O'Connor.

"Oh, and you won't have to worry about the lieutenant."

"I wasn't worried, sir," O'Connor said respectfully. "But he shoulda been."

"Right, then," the colonel responded after staring a brief few seconds into O'Connor's steady blue eyes.

The troop train ride to Calais was uneventful. Sitting on wooden benches, the wounded, gassed, burned, and shell-shocked British and Irish soldiers were returning home to lives of wretched recovery. Families anxiously awaited the arrival of whole human beings, knowing full well that their hopes would be dashed against crutches, bandaged heads, blinded eyes or vacant stares coupled with nervous laughter and somber, deadened expressions. Such would be the spoils of the war won by those who fought what the politicians were calling the war to end all wars.

The small train chugged its way south across the frozen French countryside. Three cars that carried horses and cannons followed four train cars directly behind the engine that were filled with scores of war-weary soldiers.

A gaunt Jack O'Connor stood at the open door of the third car. A group of three soldiers playing cards and huddled at the rear of the car with its large sliding door.

"Hey, Mick! Close that fuggin' door!"

Another soldier chimed in. "Yah, it's freezin', you stupid potato head."

O'Connor turned and glared at them. His face was smudged with clay from some distant battlefield and the gray mud also matted his hair. The dark circles under his eyes made him look like a walking dead man who had not fallen over yet, but there was fire in his blood-shot eyes.

He slid the door closed and slowly walked to the soldiers. He positioned himself between them and their Lee-Enfield 0.303-inch rifles leaning against the side of the train car.

A sergeant who sat alone near the rifles stood up and looked first at the group and then directly at O'Connor.

"No trouble now, lads. You, there, what's your name?"

"O'Connor, sergeant. Jack O'Connor."

"Well, Mr. O'Connor, you look a little frayed at the edges. The boys meant no harm. Anyone who fights the Krauts is okay by us. Right, lads?"

The three soldiers looked up from their poker hands and glared at O'Connor, who reached under his coat and put his hand on his knife.

"Hold on, there. Why not tell us where you're headin', O'Connor?"

"Home, sergeant."

"Back to your Irish farm then, eh? Or maybe to Dublin?"

O'Connor didn't respond, but looked nonchalantly down at the three soldiers.

One of the soldiers looked up from his cards.

"We was talking earlier, O'Connor. You're not carrying a rifle."

"Didja lose it to some Kraut, Mick?"

The soldiers laughed at the non-joke. O'Connor's eyes narrowed and his nostrils flared slightly.

"So now, Mick, our country was good enough to equip you with a rifle. Where is it?"

"Never had one after I hit the Rhine."

A soldier with an almost unintelligible Cockney accent said, "What were you, a cook's potato peeler?"

All three soldiers laughed, plus others on the opposite side of the train car. O'Connor waited for the laughter to subside before he responded.

"None of you brave Brits'd volunteer, so I snuck behind the Kraut lines at night. All I had were a pistol and …"

He pulled his knife out and held it close to his chest so just the three soldiers and the sergeant could see it and lowered his voice.

"… this here pig sticker. It'll cut a Brit throat just as clean through as a Kraut one."

"Hold on, mate," the sergeant said. "The boys didn't know. Just put it away like a good lad."

The sergeant leaned over and spoke softly to the three playing poker, who then look frightened. They hastily gathered up their playing cards and sat back.

"Killing's over, Mr. O'Connor," the sergeant said in a calm voice. We're all going home, so let's just leave it at that, shall we?"

O'Connor thought for a moment, considered the odds, and then slid the knife back into the sheath under his coat. He walked over to the closed sliding door and leaned his back against it. It was too dark for the others to see the beads of cold sweat on his face, or to see him reach up and wipe them away. Since he couldn't kill, he stifled the scream to rid himself of the urge.

Except for a few barbed wire scrapes and heel blisters, O'Connor was going home unscathed, physically and emotionally. His mind was intact, possibly because, rather than only seeing his mates bodies torn apart by bombs and artillery shells, O'Connor had been the cause of death and mayhem to scores of Austrian soldiers in their own encampments. Their deaths from the razor-sharp blade he skillfully wielded, while for naught in O'Connor's mind, had been his job, a job he didn't hate, but one he didn't love either. It was what it was – a way to create panic in the Germans, to force their soldiers to fear the dark and lose precious sleep.

Stiff and sore from the train ride, O'Connor hiked with the others toward the docks and checked in at the camp that the Brits had set up for soldiers done with war. He found an empty bunk in a tent close to the front gate, dumped his gear at the foot of it and lay down, falling into a fitful sleep.

Rising early the next day and the next, he dressed in the clean uniform given to him to a nice elderly Red Cross woman and wandered the streets of the French port waiting for the troop transport ship. The sights and sounds assaulted his senses enough to bury his memories, but the quiet of the nights, punctuated by the occasional barking dog and cursing from some drunken fight, allowed dark memories and heartaches to rush into his consciousness.

Whenever he first closed his eyes, he saw his ma and siblings lying in their house, his da shot and dying, digging the graves with the little bodies lined up, getting shot, running until his lungs burned, waking up in pain, putting little bodies in their graves … He willed his eyes to open each night to stop the flood of horror.

Eyes wide open in the darkness, images of what he had done the past months rushed before him like a raging river. Killing had come so naturally that now that talent scared him, made him shudder at what he was capable of doing to another human being. But the Germans weren't really human, were they; animals trying to conquer the World. That's what the Brit drill instructors had told the recruits. It's easier to kill a subhuman than a real person, he had told himself over and over.

On the third morning in the French port, he decided that feeling like a monster himself could only cause self loathing, so he accepted his past, embraced what he had done to save the World from German domination, and vowed to never kill another human being … unless he had to.

The resolution brought him relief from visions of the soldiers he had killed except for the youngest one. The lad's expressions when he had gone for his gun and then the shocked look as O'Connor slashed his throat would never completely retreat.

Acceptance brought another change. O'Connor felt like bathing and shaving. In the early morning, just before dawn, he marched to the lavatory tent, removed his skivvies, climbed into the makeshift field shower in the holding camp, and washed away the grime of war.

After shaving his weeks old beard and in a clean uniform, he felt almost human. As he walked back to his tent, he heard the loud, garbled announcement coming from the camp loudspeakers.

"Ship" was the only word he could make out, but it was enough. He ran back to the tent, pushed his way through the other soldiers gathering their gear, and rushed out the camp gate onto the street that led to the dock.

O'Connor watched the ship steam into port at Calais, and with the others on the dock, stared in amazement as the ship came in too fast and rammed the dock, knocking over sailors on board waiting to throw over the mooring lines. One poor bastard was tossed head over heels and, mercifully, ended up spread eagle on his back on top of a pile of folded up old command tents heading to Dover for repair.

Once the soldiers on the dock realized the man was unhurt, they laughed and cheered his successful dive. Their laughter got louder once the flying sailor yelled to them that the ship's captain recently graduated at the bottom of his class from the new Pangbourne Nautical College.

Their laughter grew into the joyous cheers of soldiers arriving at the realization that they were finally going home – alive.

-5-

CÚIG

The old steamer the British Navy converted to a troop carrier made the 47 nautical miles to Dover in just over four hours, barely long enough for O'Connor to get into five fights, threatened with death by several bystanders, and nearly thrown overboard by a gang of British sailors before they were stopped by two Irish lads.

Debarking took O'Connor and the other soldiers another hour, double what it had taken them to board ship in Calais.

O'Connor and his new mates, a couple of retired infantrymen scarred by mustard gas, who hailed from Limerick, caught a train to Holyhead on England's west coast. There they found passage with a patriotic Irish fisherman who just happened to be headed back to Dun Laoghaire to buy some fine Irish linen and sweaters.

He traveled with the lads to Limerick, where they parted ways. He was jealous of the welcome they received from their families and he declined their many invitations to supper because he knew the jocularity around the tables would only serve to make him lonelier and sadder, to miss his family even more. His friends' families looked puzzled and more than a little miffed as they watched him hike down the road, duffle bag slung over his shoulder, arm over his head waving goodbye.

O'Connor walked another day until the truth of his

freedom from war lifted the fog of war. The farther he walked, the deeper the war recessed, the lighter his burden felt. He was home. Alive. Unharmed.

Each day of his journey he stopped whenever he reached a village with an inn that offered weary travelers hot food and Guinness and a room with a passably comfortable bed. No matter what the evening's fare, it always tasted better than army rations and camp food. Seeing his uniform, the old men in every pub would ask him to recount his war experiences, but as most soldiers who have seen the horrors of battle, O'Connor would politely decline. Then, to change the subject, he would buy a round of drinks and ask the men to sing their favorite Irish ballads. After the third or fourth song, usually "Molly Malone" or "All For Me Grog," O'Connor would quietly go to his room so he could enjoy a full night's sleep. The following morning, he would arise at first light, dress hurriedly, and rush outside to breathe the fresh morning air and watch the full sunrise over the green fields of his beloved homeland. His mood improved each day until the last morning when he knew he would reach home mid-day. A pall came over him that he could not shake off.

O'Connor stopped at the gate to the small cottage. His British Army uniform was clean, but his boots were muddy and scuffed from four days of walking. He scanned the scene with sadness as memories flooded through him like water through a leaking dam that finally bursts.

Junk was strewn in the yard, an overturned milk bucket teemed with dead maggots. A few snow-white geese waddled around, pecking at the grass.

The dilapidated cottage sat at the edge of a green pasture. Behind the house in a field green with spring grass sat a small horse-drawn riding plow, tipped over.

O'Connor swallowed hard and opened the gate. The geese scattered from the path leading to the front door. O'Connor grabbed the door handle and rattled the door, which was secured by a rusty padlock. He shook his head at his own stupid futility and walked to the nearest window and peered in.

Through the dirty window he could see that his boyhood home was empty. He stood transfixed as the bloody ghosts of his mother and siblings slowly materialized on the dark-stained floor. Tears welled up in his eyes and the bitter taste of angry bile rose in his throat.

O'Connor cursed and the ghosts disappeared, but his anger did not. He had seen his father die at their hands, lost his whole family, everyone he loved, and had fought for the bastards, doing the dirty killing none of them would do. In time, he vowed, he would get his revenge when the Brits least expected it.

O'Connor walked angrily from the house. The geese scattered. He picked up the milk bucket and threw it through the cottage window and headed past the barn to the graves he had dug. He was relieved to see that they were undisturbed. He gathered some sticks and using old twine he found in the barn, he fashioned crosses that he stuck at what he remembered was the head of each grave.

O'Connor said no prayer, unless cursing God could be considered praying.

"What kind of god does this to innocents," he muttered. "If you're there, damn you to Hell," he yelled.

Standing next to his mother's grave with angry tears flooding down his cheeks, O'Connor stripped off his uniform jacket and tossed it as far away as he could. He sailed his cap after it. Done being the good soldier, he grabbed his knapsack and tromped up the road the way he came. Yes, he thought, vengeance will be mine.

He roamed Ireland for five months after visiting the farm. He loved hiking on the winding roads, the smell of the peat bogs, and the sight of low stone fences dividing one farm, one pasture from the next. It began to heal his emotions, but nothing would remove the scars.

Along the way, farmers would most often offer him a meal of cooked oats and eggs. Some just gave him tea. To their credit they complimented him on his service during the war. Some, though, accused him under their breath of being a traitor to the Irish Independence movement. Most, though, had been so terrified that the Germans would invade England and Ireland, that they appreciated anyone who helped defeat them.

Every town of any size offered O'Connor a good bare-knuckle fighting opportunity where he could make enough money to feed himself until he got to the next town. There was always a local bully who thought himself tough enough to step into the ring with him. They were always wrong.

Every village pub was a good source of a pint of Guinness, some wild music, and a sad ballad or two. As the months went by, O'Connor saw the poverty beneath the surface of Ireland's beauty. Despite what the Brits told the world, Ireland was still starving and children were still dying. And like most Irish, O'Connor felt powerless to stop the tragedy.

One day, as he huddled under a bridge to escape a downpour, he realized that wandering the countryside aimlessly was a waste of his life. He needed a purpose and that purpose was to live a life of peace. To do that, he would need to buy his family's farm, which meant he needed money. He needed to leave Ireland and get to America, a land of riches beyond belief, a land where anyone could become a millionaire.

When the rain stopped, he put his plan into action. He would travel to Killybegs and sign on with the first freighter bound for New York. The walk would be long, but he knew he would be able to find work as a stevedore and earn enough for passage to America. And so he walked his way north through Ireland from Killarney, stopping only to fight and sleep. Most meals he ate as he walked, or only when he rested briefly.

On the tenth day, O'Connor walked to the top of a stone-scattered hill and looked down on Killybegs Harbour, with its lighthouse and streets all leading to the water. Four large freighters sat docked there, gently rising and falling with the waves. As he walked down the road into the picturesque town he picked the one that looked the most seaworthy. 'There's my ticket to America,' he thought.

An hour later, O'Connor stood on the dock as burly stevedores off loaded large wooden containers, filled, he guessed, with large bags of sugar, or boxes of cigars. He didn't have the slightest idea what they contained and could not care less. His real interest was the huge bundles of fine Irish wool and linen, wrapped in cargo nets that he would offer to load by himself for passage.

"Your boys look worn out," O'Connor said to the burly dock boss standing at a makeshift podium next to the gangplank. "I'll put aboard your load."

"Not hiring," the man said looking down at papers on the podium.

"No charge," O'Connor responded. "I'll work for passage."

The man still didn't look up. "We don't need no one," he said.

"I'll hoist your goods myself, and then do whatever shite job on board for the full trip over."

The man finally looked up and smiled slyly. "If you can hoist a bale of wool onto the deck by yourself, I may be able to use you," he said disdainfully.

O'Connor dropped his knapsack on the dock and grabbing a hoist line with a heavy iron hook at the end, jumped onto the top of the closest bale, hooked the large rings that held together the cargo net's four corners, and jumped down.

A crowd of deck hands stopped to watch when O'Connor yelled to a deck hand leaning over the ship's rail to ready the hoist rope. When the man had the rope in his hands, O'Connor sprinted up the gang plank, grabbed the rope and hurled himself over the side of the ship onto the dock. His momentum carried him to a stanchion and the bale of wool lurched off the dock. O'Connor quickly wrapped the line around the stanchion and pulled with all his might. The bale gradually rose until it reached the ship's main deck near the cargo hold. One of the deck hands grabbed the cargo net and swung it over the cargo hold. He gave O'Connor the sign to lower the load, and O'Connor gradually threaded the rope hand over hand until it went slack.

One man on the dock began to clap slowly, and he was soon joined by the others. Ignoring their accolades, O'Connor sauntered over to the dock boss, looked him in the eye, and said, "Where do I bunk?"

The trip over was smooth, save for one nasty storm off the coast of Greenland. The captain had taken the shorter route north by northwest to avoid long nights in the mid-Atlantic. He knew rough seas were probable, but wanted to stay within a day's sail of land during the passage. The ship and crew were well prepared for the storm. As gale force winds drove the ocean into a frenzy of 40-foot waves that crashed over the deck, all hands knew their survival depended on their training and the captain's experience. After a rough night during which men stayed below decks and the ship headed into the waves, the seas calmed and the mood onboard lightened.

O'Connor experienced only one unpleasantness during the voyage. He had been swabbing the forecastle deck when a burly crew chief, who was a head taller than O'Connor, told him in a guttural Cockney brogue, to stop mopping and follow him below to the engine room.

"I've the perfect job fer ya, Mick," he sneered.

The engine room felt to O'Connor like the inside of an oven and the air smelled of grease, sweat, and rotting fish.

"The cap'n says you're to clean out the bilge," he ordered O'Connor, barely able to disguise a chortle. "Got to earn yer keep."

The man handed him a large bucket that held a smaller scoop bucket with a handle welded to one side.

"Use the small bucket to scoop out the bilge and put it into the larger bucket," he explained, "then tote the large bucket topside and throw it off the stern."

As O'Connor lifted the grated access cover the full stench of the bilge water hit his nose causing him to retch slightly. He took a deep breath and bent down on his hands and knees. As he did so, the big Brit shoved him into the bilge. O'Connor landed hands first, barely able to keep his head from going into the brackish water.

The big man's laughter set off a chain reaction. O'Connor pushed himself up and out of the bilge. With hands dripping with saltwater, seagull shit and sailor piss, he grabbed the bilge cover and shoved it at the larger man's knees. As the man fell backward, O'Connor launched himself up from his kneeling position, and using his fists, hardened and scarred by scores of bare-knuckle fights, caught the big man in the throat and the chin. The combination felled the large man like a lumberjack felling a tree with the final swing of an axe.

The laughter stopped. O'Connor grabbed the big man's ankles and dragged him to the open bilge. He shoved the man's lower torso into the bilge water, leaving his arms and head on the deck. He wedged the cover under the man's neck to keep him from sliding into the water.

"When he comes to," O'Connor said to the boiler tenders, "tell him I'll be topside if he wants to go another round."

Somehow the big Brit was able to avoid seeing O'Connor the rest of the voyage. They didn't see each other again until they docked in New York Harbor.

-6-

sé

Seen from the deck of a ship, the Americans' Statue of Liberty was indeed impressive, thought O'Connor. He had heard talk of the sights of the harbor onboard, but the sailors' descriptions didn't do the large statue justice. Something inside him stirred with awe and doubt. Would this be his new home? Would he ever see his beloved Ireland again? Could he survive by fighting? The doubts plagued him just as the beauty and grandeur of New York impressed him.

Once the ship docked, the work of offloading its cargo began. A hundred men lined up on the dock waiting to learn if they would work today. Most were Irish, but many were Italians and Polish and German Jews. All had strong backs and knew what work was needed before being told. Both qualities qualified them to work offloading cargo. Most had worked together one day or another. But the ship's country of origin generally dictated who worked that day. This day Irish worked before Italians, and they both worked before the Jews. It was the way of their world.

As he transferred cargo from the ship's hold onto the dock below, O'Connor was engulfed in the odors of the port. Diesel fuel and saltwater were the most prevalent, but occasionally the smell of fresh seafood drifted past, along with the faint aroma of garlic and cooking meat from distant kitchens. The combination would stay with him the rest of his life, so that whenever he smelled saltwater and diesel fuel, he would remember this day and another event that again changed his life forever.

O'Connor had gathered his meager belongings from the crew's quarters and climbed the ladders two levels to the main deck. There he saw the captain and the bursar. As the bursar handed a departing sailor his pay for the voyage, the captain would say something to the sailor, who either smiled or looked stoic, depending on the captain's words.

It was near dark when O'Connor collected his pay, and as he stuffed it into his left front pants pocket, the captain said to him, "You're a good hand, Mick, but you nearly killed one of my regulars. Good luck in America."

It was the captain's way of telling O'Connor not to come back for the return voyage. O'Connor didn't care. He hadn't planned to, but he smiled at the man and thanked him for the passage.

As O'Connor walked down the gang plank, he noticed a small group of men standing off to the side at the head of the pier. When he walked closer, he saw that each of the men carried a large club. Standing in their midst was the large Brit he had beaten.

O'Connor stopped walking as soon as he realized what was about to happen. He put down his grip on the dock, reached inside and pulled out his combat knife. He knew the odds were against him, but he also knew that while these men may be thugs, none were probably trained killers and bare-knuckle boxers. It would be an old fashioned Donnybrook, but with a deadly conclusion.

O'Connor left his grip on the dock and walked toward the gang.

"Bring your friends to protect you?" he yelled at the Brit.

"There'll be no sucker punch this time. They're going to

soften you up a bit, Mick," the man yelled back, "then I'm going to finish you off."

O'Connor kept walking. As he got within arm's length, the first man swung his brickbat at O'Connor, who ducked and buried his knife in the man's belly just below his rib cage. With a turn of the knife and an upward thrust, he bisected the man's heart.

Just then, all hell broke loose behind the gang. Hit from behind, two of the men fell in clumps. Seeing their numbers reduced by three, two others dropped their clubs and sprinted off to the side of the dock and disappeared between stacks of cargo.

This left the big Brit standing between O'Connor and a group of men armed with knives and large spiked clubs.

"Seems your friends abandoned you, Brit," O'Connor said to the man. "I beat you once and I ain't got a reason to kill ya', lest you give me one. Maybe you should follow your brave men and go drink a few pints before you get yourself hurt."

The big man took a step toward O'Connor but stopped when he saw O'Connor's bloody knife and heard the sound behind him. The second gang's members were pounding the ends of their clubs on the dock in unison. It was a menacing, primeval thwacking, and it rattled him. He dropped his club and slowly walked sideways in the direction his own two gang members had run. He disappeared down an alley. O'Connor never saw him again.

He bent down and wiped the blade of his combat knife on the pants leg of the dead man, slipped his knife into his belt and walked back to the middle of the dock, picked up his grip, and turned around. He came belt buckle to face with a short, stocky red-haired man with a full red beard, short muscular arms, and a big grin. He held up his hand, not to shake O'Connor's hand, but to give him an oily paper package.

Without a word, the little man turned and rejoined his crew, as all of them walked off into the night.

Puzzled, O'Connor put down his grip and untied the twine that held the small package together. Inside he found an official immigration certificate, a dockworkers union card, and 500 dollars in worn 20 dollar notes. As he looked through the contents, a small piece of paper fluttered to the ground. O'Connor picked it up and unfolded it as he straightened up. The only thing on the paper was an address – 17 Assembly Road.

'And where the fock do you suppose THAT is,' he thought.

Shoving the papers in his pockets and picking up his belongings, O'Connor walked off the dock and into the port area, ever watchful for an attack that could come from behind any building, the next dark alley, or around any corner.

He walked through the night, but as daylight began to filter between the tall buildings, O'Connor realized two things. One, this New York was larger than even Dublin; and two, he was exhausted from walking and being on edge all night. Not since the war had he felt this kind of mental exhaustion. He wasn't afraid. He could handle almost any attack, but being ready for a fight at any moment had left him tired.

As the adrenaline worked its way out of his blood, O'Connor looked for a place to rest. Two blocks later he found a decent looking hotel, checked in for two nights, and paid the four dollars the desk clerk demanded in advance.

O'Connor had barely stretched out on the bed in his second floor room when, fully clothed, he fell asleep.

He slept all that day and through the night, rising only to walk down the hall and relieve himself in the cramped communal commode.

In his dreams, he saw flashes of war. Cried for his dead mother and sisters. Held his dying father in his young arms. The worst of the horrors, what caused him night sweats, was the image of the German boy in a uniform that was a size too large, which he should never have been forced to wear. The boy's eyes pleaded for mercy and then hardened into bravado right before O'Connor's dream self severed the boy's head from his body. Blackness followed. Then red and black demons carrying flaming tridents sat on his chest.

He lurched awake. After what seemed like only a few minutes, hunger and thirst fully awakened him before sunlight streamed through the lace curtains. It was mid-morning. Time to find 17 Assembly Road.

-7-

seacht

O'Connor clomped down the hotel's carpeted stairs and threw his room key onto the front desk. The same clerk greeted him with a sarcastic look. O'Connor faced the man, noticing his rumpled banded collar shirt, which hadn't seen the inside of a wash tub in weeks. Speaking slowly and deliberately trying to hide his Irish brogue, he asked the fellow where 17 Assembly Road was.

"Brooklyn," was all the man said.

"Where might that be," O'Connor asked.

"Ask a copper, I ain't no tour guide."

Rather than grabbing the man by the neck and shaking him like a ratter with his catch, O'Connor breathed deeply and walked out the door.

Outside he scanned the street for a trolley or taxi. Seeing none, he headed up the narrow street to the closest intersection. There he found a line of taxis waiting for fares. He approached the first one, driven by a thin, scruffy man reading what appeared to be a racing form.

"Can you take me to Brooklyn," he asked the man.

"Could, but I won't," he said without looking up. "No taxis into Brooklyn."

"How do I get there," O'Connor asked.

"See that big fancy bridge over there," he said pointing north, never looking up. "Just walk across that and you'll be in Brooklyn."

Designed by John Augustus Roebling, a German immigrant, and completed in 1883, the Brooklyn Bridge spanned the East River and connected Manhattan and Brooklyn. O'Connor marveled at its size as he trekked across the expanse. The view up and down the river was spectacular, and photographers lined the railings looking and waiting for an award-winning shot. Several had their cameras set on tripods and offered pedestrians photos of themselves on the bridge for one dollar.

Once on the Brooklyn side, O'Connor asked a tall, heavyset policeman directions to 17 Assembly Road.

"Whatcha want there, Boyo," he asked O'Connor, his Irish brogue barely understandable to anyone other than another Irishman.

"They're giving me a job," O'Connor answered.

"You be careful what kind of job they give you," said the cop. He stared at O'Connor. "Now that I know your face, I'll be looking for you causing trouble."

"Where didya say this place is," O'Connor asked, ignoring the cop's threat.

"Walk south by the water and you'll find it."

O'Connor walked on the cobblestone pathway lining the East River. He marveled at the size of the buildings across the river and wondered what people who occupied them did in such tall places.

After another 20 minutes O'Connor turned down a street labeled 'Assembly Road.'

The small tin numbers nailed over a metal barn door identified 17 Assembly Road. Across the street an electric street lamp cast an eerie pale light on the cobblestones of the street. O'Connor warily looked up and down the street and listened. Seeing and hearing nothing, he rapped the butt end of his knife against the metal door … three times, paused, then twice more as he had been instructed in the note handed him by the red-headed dwarf. No response. Impatient, O'Connor repeated the coded knock.

The door opened to reveal a large man he thought he had seen before. The man motioned O'Connor in and slid the door closed. Seeing the knife, he held out his meaty plate-size palm and wriggled his fingers until O'Connor put the knife in the man's left hand. Next, the man ran his right hand down O'Connor's sides and back, then handed back his knife and turned to walk down the dark corridor.

O'Connor followed the large man, which is what he supposed he was to do even though the hulk hadn't said a word. A short walk later they entered a large room stacked floor-to-ceiling with wooden barrels. The sweet smell of beer wafted into O'Connor's nose through the odor of stale and fresh pipe tobacco smoke. Most of the barrels were marked "Canadian Whiskey." A few, close to O'Connor, carried the markings "Jameson of Dublin." He rubbed his hand over the nearest barrel.

"That's for our best customers," a voice boomed. O'Connor turned toward the voice and smiled slightly. Sitting atop a large barrel at the back center of the warehouse, was the small red-haired man who had handed him the package at the dock. He was dressed in traditional Irish garb – hobnail boots, woolen pants, and a wool vest over a striped collarless cotton flannel shirt. A bowler hat adorned with a green band rested cocked over his left eye.

"Approach," he commanded. "Glad you found us, Mr. O'Connor."

O'Connor was used to being told what to do, but he didn't like the tone in the little man's voice.

"For someone who's a wee bit like a Leprechaun," O'Connor said, "you seem to think you're a giant of a man."

The small man laughed derisively.

"You'd be surprised what a small man can do with big friends."

Several men walked toward O'Connor. The little man raised his hand to stop them.

Assessing his predicament and planning his attack, O'Connor gripped his knife.

"Relax, Mr. O'Connor," said the little man. "You can't do me any good if you're dead."

"Why am I here," O'Connor asked, "and how the feck do you know my name?"

"Elementary, my dear Watson," the little man said quoting the popular penny-novel detective, Sherlock Holmes.

"You have friends in high places who need certain favors only you can provide."

"What friends?"

"In due time, Mick. In due time. Come sit down so we can discuss your future here and in Chicago."

O'Connor walked toward the man who motioned for O'Connor to sit on a smaller barrel and handed him a flask of Jameson's finest.

"I'd rather have beer for breakfast if you don't mind," O'Connor said.

"Of course. Bring our guest a mug," the little man commanded to a man standing next to a keg of Guinness.

As O'Connor drank his breakfast, the diminutive man spoke in a low voice. "I had a man on board the ship who sent me word about your incident. He was impressed with your speed and brutality, but also by your self control. These attributes can carry you far."

Just then the ship's captain walked around a stack of whiskey barrels.

"The good captain thinks you can fill a need we have for a smart boyo in the West," the little man said. "Isn't that right, Captain."

"Right, Mr. Shannon."

"We have been consigned to do a serious job in a place called Bismarck for some friends who, quite frankly, need a job of their own in order to survive this depression we're in. In turn, they are willing to give me certain control over the import of my entertainment businesses in Chicago."

"And where would this Chicago be," O'Connor asked.

"Just a short train ride away," Shannon said. Laughter broke out in the warehouse.

"A short few days train ride," he said.

"And what am I to do in this Chicago?"

"I believe it involves working in a slaughterhouse for a time, and generally laying low until your employer decides when the time is right to do what he needs doing," Shannon said.

"What do I get out of this?" O'Connor asked.

"Your life, for one thing, and more money than you can spend in two lifetimes."

"Sounds like trouble," said O'Connor.

"We know you're no stranger to trouble," Shannon said.

"I ain't, but that don't mean I want more."

"I believe you want to live peacefully back home. Isn't that why you came to America? To make enough money to buy your old farm?"

"'Tis."

"And just how were you going to earn enough in this

country?"

"Boxing."

Again laughter broke out in the warehouse.

Shannon stood up and stretched. "You and every other Irish punk with two fists," he said to O'Connor after the laughter died down. "But if that's you're calling, then you'll surely get your fill of it in Chicago, but not here," Shannon said.

"The train leaves tomorrow morning at 7:28. When you get to the platform, say my name to the conductor. He'll let you board and tell you where to sit."

"And just why should I do anything you tell me to do," O'Connor said.

"If you don't, Mr. O'Connor, you won't live to regret it."

O'Connor shrugged. He bristled at the threat and tensed for a fight, but the idea of a job and the freedom to do some one-on-one bare-knuckle fighting was enough for him to take the wiser road.

Grip in hand he backed away from Shannon and his thugs until he thought he was a safe distance away, and then he turned and sauntered out of the warehouse to show them he wasn't afraid. He kept his right hand wrapped around the handle of his knife just in case. He walked cautiously, vigilant for attacks from every dark alley, until he came to a decent-looking hotel, paid for his one night's stay, and fell quickly asleep in his room on the single sagging bed, knife held on his chest.

-8-

OCHT

The following morning, O'Connor rose in the pre-dawn darkness, quickly packed his few belongings, and headed on foot across Manhattan. He hailed the first taxi he saw and told the driver to take him as fast as possible to Grand Central Terminal.

He jumped out of the taxi, threw the fare at the cabbie and hurried into the station at 7:04. He raced through the morning crowd to the boarding area where he searched up and down the gates for his train, spying it at last and sprinted to the first passenger car. He approached the first conductor, a short, rotund man with slicked back hair under his conductor's cap and a tight-fitting uniform. When O'Connor got close, he said "Shannon" to him. The man looked up at him as if he was daft, but pointed down the platform toward another conductor.

When he said "Shannon" to the second conductor, the man handed him a ticket.

"Two cars down there's a small compartment with a brass window frame on the door. Stay in there and don't come out until we get to Chicago."

As he boarded the 20th-Century Limited, which would carry him to Chicago's LaSalle Street Station, O'Connor was amazed at the train's opulence, unlike any troop carrier or Irish train he had been on. Rich wood and heavy curtains adorned the passageway. The floor was covered in what appeared to be woolen carpet with a floral design.

After passing through two sets of doors, he arrived at the car where his compartment was located. He found the right door, pushed it open, and could barely fit his large frame inside.

He had passed a smaller room, which he supposed was the loo, and decided he would use it instead of the spittoon in the corner of his compartment. O'Connor sat down in a seat by the window, and figured that the seat opposite would fold down somehow into a bed on which he would have to curl his large frame 12 hours later so he could get some sleep during the 18 to 20 hour ride.

For most of the daylight hours, O'Connor stared out the window and marveled in the vast expanse of the countryside and the water, which he thought must still be the ocean because he could not see an opposite shore.

He knew absolutely nothing about the lay of this land to which so many of his countrymen had emigrated. For whatever other reasons, most left Ireland because they faced little prospect of work at home, hunger and starvation, and an oppressive British government that kept Ireland's Catholic people squarely under its thumb. At least in America a man was free to make a living, even become a millionaire, so they thought. In reality, it offered little to its average citizens, except for massive government programs for the poor and unemployed, and high taxes on the rich and employed Americans to pay for them.

O'Connor looked out at rolling hills and dozed off when the scenery became monotonous. During those brief times, he thought about home and how, no matter how long it took him, he would someday return to Ireland and buy his family farm. They can have this large country with its large problems. He had been a soldier, had fought for the Brits. Through the war and strife, he had never lost his love for Ireland and his longing for a peaceful life.

When the train slowed east of Chicago, O'Connor awoke. The industrial buildings with their smokestacks belching gray filth were a blur, as were the stockyards and slaughterhouses. It seemed like hours before the train crawled into the station and lurched to a stop.

O'Connor gathered his coat, hat, and grip and slid open the door to his sleeper room. Other passengers rushed by him to the doors of the sleeper cars. He waited for a break and entered the stream.

LaSalle Street Station bustled with activity. O'Connor wended his way from the trains to the LaSalle Street exit. Other people got jostled in the rush to get out of the station. Not O'Connor. The war and his hand-to-mouth bare-knuckle fights across Ireland had hardened his body, which had grown to a full six feet four inches in height. His height and broad shoulders caused the crowd to swerve around him like a rushing stream flows around a boulder.

As he exited the station through the revolving brass door, O'Connor looked up and down LaSalle Street before approaching the taxi stand. When he turned his head to the north, a tall man standing by the nearest pillar casually stepped behind it and raised his newspaper so only the top of his head shown over the pages. He was dressed head to toe in black. His black fedora sat atop slicked-back black hair. He had a swarthy complexion, full, neatly trimmed black beard, and a black overcoat covered his frame and reached down to his shiny black riding boots. Had O'Connor spotted him, he might have thought the man was an undertaker, but the man purposefully evaded O'Connor's gaze.

Every taxi O'Connor approached showed "On Duty", but the drivers waved him off. Frustrated, he tried several before finding one that allowed him to get in the back seat.

As O'Connor shoe-horned into the taxi, the driver lowered his newspaper and nodded slightly in the direction of the taxi stand while keeping his eyes glued to the newspaper. No one noticed except the two men for whom it was intended.

~9~

NAOI

"I want a clean boarding house," O'Connor said to the taxi driver.

The driver nodded and pulled out into traffic.

"What brings ya here, Mick," asked the driver in a voice hoarse from yelling out his window, which he did with annoying regularity in the first few minutes of O'Connor's ride.

"Looking for work," O'Connor said.

"You and about a million other Irish," the man yelled back at O'Connor.

O'Connor stared out the taxi window at the passing buildings. He had enough money to last him a few months, but he didn't want to run low before finding work. Money comforted him. Running out made him edgy. He preferred comfort.

The taxi driver suddenly pulled over. The car sat next to the curb for a few seconds before another taxi pulled up behind it and two men jumped out and stood on either side of O'Connor's cab.

"Time to get out," the driver said.

O'Connor was confused. One of the men handed the driver a small manila envelope across the front seat.

"Out," the man barked at O'Connor, who looked toward the street for an escape route, only to see the other man standing by that door.

Both men opened their coats just enough to reveal their pistols, dashing any hope of winning a knife fight with the two.

Exasperated, O'Connor sighed. The man standing on the sidewalk opened the taxi door, and O'Connor slammed the car's door against him. As he stumbled backward he drew and pointed his pistol at O'Connor. The taxi sped off, and the other man ran onto the sidewalk with his gun pointed at O'Connor's back.

O'Connor was preparing to drive his fist into the nose of the man in front of him when a black 1922 Packard Phaeton roared to a halt behind the second taxi. The tall man dressed in black jumped out of the driver's door and rushed toward O'Connor.

"No need for violence," Mr. O'Connor," he said. O'Connor stopped his fist in mid-swing and looked toward the man in black. The blow from behind caught O'Connor at the base of his skull and everything went black.

When he came to, he was lying face down on a lumpy thin mattress. O'Connor lifted up his head to look around with blurred vision. A voice from across the room said, "So you've come around."

O'Connor blinked his eyes several times and his vision cleared enough to focus on a large black blob in the opposite corner of the room.

"I thought my man had killed you," the blob said.

"Feels like he did," O'Connor said, gently rubbing the knot on his head.

O'Connor lowered his head onto the mattress. The throbbing subsided, but nausea overcame him and he turned his head over the edge of the mattress just in time to vomit in the trash can that had been placed within reach.

"Usually happens," said the blob. "When you're through, we'll talk."

The blob got taller when it floated toward O'Connor. He blinked his eyes again and the blob became a tall man dressed all in black. The man handed O'Connor a flask.

"Drink," he commanded.

O'Connor hesitated, his stomach still roiling from the blow to his head, but he took a pull from the flask and then fought to keep the burning liquid flowing down.

"You should stop being so damn belligerent, Boyo."

"Who the feck are you," O'Connor asked the man after he choked down another pull of the whiskey.

"I can be your best friend," the man said quietly, "or your worst nightmare. Your choice."

"I don't understand."

"Do what I ask you to do and we'll get on just fine."

"Depends on whatchyer asking," O'Connor said, his voice getting stronger.

The man sat down on a chair next to the bed. He pulled out a pocket knife and nonchalantly carved his fingernails. "I need you to work at my stockyard during the day and in one of my other businesses at night," he said without looking up from his fingers.

"Stockyard! Feck off!"

"You'll have a fine job so you're legitimate."

"What else," O'Connor asked.

"I have a young partner in the refreshment business who needs help cornering the market, let's say."

"And …?"

"And he needs someone with your special talents to discuss other business opportunities with his competition."

"What's this fella's name?"

"His name is of no concern," the man snapped. "You just be where I tell you to be when I tell you to be there."

"In the meantime?"

"Tomorrow you'll be at the Four Deuces at midnight. Any taxi driver will know where it is. The manager there will have a small job for you."

"After that?"

"The following morning, go to the main entrance of the stockyards. A woman there will tell you where to go."

"What's this job I'm to do?"

"You'll be handling the livestock most of the time. Sometime you'll be on the killing line."

Wonderful, O'Connor thought.

"Where am I?"

"You're at a lovely boarding house in Canaryville."

"And the stockyard?"

"The stockyards are just west of here."

The man rose from the chair. "Any questions, Mr. O'Connor?"

"Just one. When do I get to kill the fella who gave me this knot behind me ear?"

The man put on his grey goatskin gloves. "Get something to eat, then rest," he said as he opened the door. "You have a busy day tomorrow."

He left and quietly closed the door behind him.

The following morning, O'Connor rose early, before the streets of Chicago came alive. His head still hurt, but a full night's rest had revived him and he needed breakfast. His meal the night before had consisted of a stale sandwich and watery soup at the Saint Nicholas Catholic Mission two blocks away. Afterward, he had walked slowly back to the boarding house, gotten his key, and for the first time in what seemed like years, took off his clothes before climbing into bed.

This morning he wanted a diner that served large meals and strong coffee. He walked west toward the stockyards and noticed a large diner on a side street several blocks from the main gate to the stockyards.

The place was crowded, but he found a stool at the counter. Just as he sat down, a waitress put a cup in front of him and filled it with coffee.

She smiled, then hustled away.

O'Connor drank his coffee and casually looked around the diner. He had seen some Negroes heading toward the stockyards, but there were none in the diner. The place looked like it could have been in any town in Europe. Everywhere he looked sat men with olive skin and black hair, or pale skin and blonde, red or black hair. No Negroes and no women patrons. That was okay with him; he had never spent any time with Negroes, so he was ambivalent about them. And he didn't understand women, nor did he know what to say to them when he hadn't paid them to spend time with him. So it was just as well he didn't need to make conversation with one.

The waitress, an olive-skinned woman in her mid-twenties, kept his coffee cup filled. On her third trip to refill his cup, she stood behind the counter in front of him, pencil poised over the ticket pad, and stared at him, which made him uncomfortable until he realized she was going to ask what he wanted, so he ordered. She wrote on the pad and without a word, turned and shoved the ticket up into the carousel at the kitchen window. O'Connor didn't even need to talk to her after he had ordered the breakfast special, so when she slid his platter onto the counter, he ate his bacon, eggs, and flapjacks in silence.

He returned to the diner several Sundays, when he wasn't busy with "the business." Every time the routine was the same—same seat at the counter, same attractive waitress, same silent, attentive service. The only difference was the breakfast special—some days thick bacon, some days a large slab of ham.

After his fourth breakfast visit, she left a ticket by his empty plate like she did every other time. But on a second blank ticket she had written "noon" in a beautiful script. O'Connor picked up both tickets, went to the till, paid her for the breakfast and handed her back the blank ticket.

"Noon," he said to her. She simply smiled.

He spent the rest of that Sunday morning exploring the south side of Chicago, with its run-down buildings that punctuated the large commercial buildings and office buildings that housed, he read on their outsides, meat brokers, grain merchants, and slaughterhouse headquarters.

By noon he was back at the diner, and walked to the steps just as the waitress, black hair bouncing, walked out the door and down the steps. She smiled at him, stuck her arm through his and they strolled back to his boarding house.

They made love desperately, not talking before or after. She laid in his arms for a long time, then abruptly rose, got dressed and left without a word.

O'Connor dozed off, but awoke just as the sun was going down behind the buildings across the street. He dressed hurriedly and left the boarding house walking toward the stockyards. As he thought about that afternoon with the beautiful silent waitress, he could only shake his head and mutter to himself, "Women! Gotta luv 'em."

It wasn't until several weeks later that O'Connor cared

enough about her to ask her where she lived. She said nothing, but moved her fingers in a strange way. He didn't know how to react to her singular behavior, so he asked her another question.

"What's yer name, girl?"

She moved her fingers and mouthed a sound, something like "MAWERY."

It was then that it dawned on him that this beautiful woman was a deaf-mute.

She tried to get up from the bed, but O'Connor held her tighter in his arms.

"Mary!" he said. "Your name is Mary."

She looked at him quizzically, and then placed the fingers of her right hand against his lips.

"Mary," he said again. She smiled broadly and nodded her head.

O'Connor kissed her forehead and hugged her against his chest for a long time. In what little heart he had left, he knew the longer this went on, the harder it would be on her when he left. Today would have to be their last together, he decided.

-10-

ᴅᴇɪᴄʜ

The work at the stockyards was hard, but at least it was honest work, O'Connor reasoned. Moving cattle and hogs from holding pens up the ramps to the slaughter gates occupied his days and provided a good answer whenever some copper in his neighborhood asked him what he did all day.

He always thought the smell of his clothes was a dead giveaway, but apparently the average Irish cop on the beat wasn't the shiniest penny in the bank.

O'Connor would start his twelve-hour shift at 6:00 a.m. The whistle blew at 6:00 p.m. then he made his way back to the boarding house, stomping the manure off his work boots along the way.

After the hour-long trek, he would remove his boots and carry them up to his room where he put them in a wooden crate in the hall outside his room door, which was there just for that purpose.

The owner, one Mrs. Marlene Mickleson, had strict rules about not allowing cow or pig shit on her floors. Even so, the halls of the place reeked of the stuff because there was no way to get the stench completely off the boots or out of the clothes without burning them.

Every evening, O'Connor would change clothes, carefully hanging his coveralls near the window, and don his one good pair of wool pants and clean shoes for his evening job.

The evening work was generally not as hard as working his day job. He was more of a team member, though, than a lone worker. He and several other men, mostly Americans who had fought in the war, but a few Irish as well, visited back-alley bars, which everyone called "speakeasies" because, he found out, people only talked in hushed tones about them in public.

O'Connor and his "team" would look through the clubs to make sure the proprietor was only serving liquor and beer purchased from their employer, known only as "The Outfit."

The visits usually went smoothly, but if they encountered some other bootlegger's goods on the premises, O'Connor and company quickly smashed gaming tables, beer kegs, liquor bottles, and mirrors, using axes and long-handled sledgehammers, departing just minutes before cops raided the place based on an anonymous tip.

This unfortunate combination of events sent a clear message to the underground entertainment sectors of Chicago's economy—become a loyal customer of The Outfit, pay a premium for its liquid refreshments in high demand by a thirsty public, and you stay in business. Go rogue or buy from another supplier and you get a visit from the big Mick, your club gets ruined as does your life. Even after The Outfit's take the profits were so ridiculously high that smart operators gladly paid for their insurance.

In Chicago there were other ways to increase profits. Small, elaborately decorated and plush backrooms provided the more discerning customers with opium, heroin, and hookers with exotic tastes, all without The Outfit's knowledge.

That is, until one day, a certain hooker whose day job was working as a waitress at a diner a mile from the main entrance to the stockyards slipped a note written in beautiful script in the pants pocket of her sleeping boyfriend before she slipped out of his boardinghouse room.

O'Connor gave the note to The Outfit's second in command, a swarthy Italian with a large nose and scars on his face and neck. O'Connor never knew his name. But when they were out of earshot, the other men called him "Scarface." O'Connor thought it was a fitting moniker and wondered how he got the scars, but he never cared much because the rumor was that the man was leaving Chicago.

The information in the note raised O'Connor's stature in The Outfit. Instead of being just one of the smash and trash thugs, O'Connor was charged with scouting out speakeasies to find any that were disloyal or were providing entertainment other that booze and broads. He dressed in fine clothes provided by his employer and pretended to be a wealthy importer of European leather goods and fine Parisian perfumes. The ruse allowed him to visit backrooms where he could detect the unmistakable odor of burning opium.

When he reported back to the warehouse The Outfit called home, he would schedule the raid, pick the men, and go with the wrecking crew. After giving them time to wreak havoc in the front of the place, he would find the nearest phone booth and report the speakeasy to the nearest police precinct. Then, if the cops weren't on the take, they would raid the place. If they were on the take, there would be no raid by the boys in blue.

After waiting a half hour without sirens or screeching cop cars, O'Connor would place a second call. To the Feds. That always brought action. Just as he and his men were leaving the area, Eliot Ness and his legalized thugs would swoop in and arrest proprietors and customers alike. The Feds didn't know who had preceded them in the raid, but they liked having much of their work done for them, so they never tried too hard to find their accomplices.

O'Connor's stature in The Outfit grew until the night his crew burned down an entire city block and nearly killed everyone in the speakeasy.

The place was one of the city's finest, decorated in deep reds, navy blues, and garish gold.

Just before O'Connor strolled in, axe in hand, the band finished playing "Ain't Misbehavin'" and had clumsily segued into an off-key rendition of Muskrat Ramble. Off stage, seven chorus girls kicked up their legs as a warm up for their next fan dance. A short, chubby Al Jolson impersonator, complete with black face and wearing a tuxedo that made him look more like a penguin than the popular singer, paced nervously. His bookie's boss had forced him to perform for six months without pay to retire his gambling debt. He was going to sing "Sonny Boy" and hoped the boss would hear him put his heart into it.

The raid went as planned, but one of the bartenders had thrown an old kerosene lamp – a nostalgic light fixture on the stage close to the bar – at one of the men. He dodged it and the lamp and its flaming liquid crashed into the stage curtains. In minutes the entire basement nightclub was engulfed in flames.

O'Connor ran to the front entrance and was nearly trampled by the rushing crowd. He worked his way down the steps and stared at the mayhem. People weren't supposed to die in these raids, just get chased out and hauled off in paddy wagons.

O'Connor worked to help old women off the floor so

they could stumble up the steps and out the door. As he struggled to clear the place, the sight of the flames now engulfing the walls and ceiling stopped him cold.

The huge flames transfixed O'Connor's gaze. They hypnotized him, transporting him back to a different battle. He was in France. Men were dying around him. Horses ran out of the barn as it burned.

Someone grabbed his arm. A man yelled at him.

"O'Connor, get out!"

He realized he was in the burning speakeasy, mesmerized by the flames. He felt the tug of another hand on his arm. He looked down to see Mary's hand clamped on his forearm, pulling him toward the stairs. He came fully out of his trance and put his arm around her waist. Together they pushed their way up the stairs and out into the street. People jostled by, shoving them apart.

Just as he reached out for her, the first fire truck clanged to a halt. A fireman ran by O'Connor, obscuring his view of Mary. When he was able to look again, she had disappeared into the night.

Driven by guilt and gratitude, O'Connor searched the area around the speakeasy all night for Mary. He had never been to her room, or apartment, or wherever it was that she lived, so he couldn't go there and wait for her to thank her for saving his life … and tell her goodbye.

Finally, exhausted and drained of adrenaline, he returned to his room in the boarding house. He crashed on the bed and slept for 12 hours.

When he woke up, he realized that it was early afternoon and he had missed work at the stockyard. Showing up there now would only cause trouble and questions.

He went back to the diner. A few customers were

scattered throughout, some at the counter, most at booths. O'Connor took his usual stool at the counter and waited. A rough looking redhead came and stood in front of him.

"Whatcha havin', Hon?"

"Where's Mary?"

"Who?"

"The deaf girl."

"She don't work here no more. Came in early and got her pay, grabbed a donut, and left."

"Know where she lives?"

"Nope."

She stared at O'Connor. "Why you interested?"

"Just am, that's all."

"Want anything to eat?"

"No."

"Then you gotta leave. Bruno don't allow just sittin'."

O'Connor stood in front of the diner. He knew he had decided to never see Mary again, but he had seen her. Last night. He wanted to thank her for saving his life. That's all. Searching for her was futile because she didn't want to be found, he reasoned.

He took a deep breath, slowly blew the air out of pursed lips, turned and walked toward The Outfit's warehouse.

"Women," he muttered.

In an alley across the street from the diner, the man dressed in all black, stood in the shadows watching O'Connor walk away. He had been watching O'Connor for some weeks. Watching from a distance. Watching from the bars of several speakeasies. Watching and listening.

-11-

AON DÉAG

"We found our man," said the man dressed in black to the man behind him. He stood stiffly, hands clasped tightly behind his back, peering at Chicago's skyline out of the window of the office on the 14th floor of the Chicago Board of Trade.

His demeanor was that of a retired British soldier of rank. He had, in fact, served the Crown during the Irish troubles and during the war. The war had been hard on him, especially one particularly gruesome trench battle during which he saw too many of his countrymen die when he commanded them to get off their bloody arses and charge behind him across no man's land. It had been a slaughter, even with saving the men he dragged back screaming and writhing in pain.

With no family to welcome him home, he had drifted into Northern Ireland, worked for a time as a policeman in Belfast where he learned to look the other way when the Orangemen caused trouble in the Catholic neighborhoods, and then, bothered by the violence, he joined the ranks of disgruntled veterans who emigrated to America, small pensions and savings depleted, hoping for a better life.

Once in America, he learned there was a certain kind of work for a former British sergeant who enjoyed enforcing orders.

Within a few days of arriving in Boston, a designer

and builder of large buildings, a transplanted Scotch-Irish architect named Clayton Andrews, recruited him through a newspaper ad in the Boston Herald.

"Live the good life in the American West. Serve at the pleasure of a loyal British subject. Bring ad and war record to Mr. C. Andrews, Chicago Board of Trade. No Negroes or Irish need apply."

Andrews had carefully looked over the man's military papers. Without looking up, he asked, "So, Stratford, tell me more about yourself."

"Not much else to tell, sir," Jasper Stratford said. "I commanded some boys in Dublin and dealt with the Irish troubles until the war. After the war I went to Belfast, then I shipped over, spent all my money getting here. Brought your ad, if you'd like to see it."

"No, no, I know you've got it. Otherwise how would you know to be here?"

"Right you are, sir."

"You can start at once," Andrews said. "Tell my secretary you're the new man. She'll give you some money and the key to a small room not far from here. Be in the waiting room at nine tomorrow morning."

"Right, sir," he said, then turned to leave.

"And Mr. Stratford," Andrews said, "Don't talk to any of the architects or draftsmen. Ever."

"Right, sir."

Here the two were seven months later discussing a task they had designed to save Andrews's architectural firm from bankruptcy.

"But we need to move fast before the Mick gets arrested or killed."

"What makes you think he'll leave Chicago," asked

Andrews from behind the desk.

Without turning around, Stratford said, "He's got no ties here. I made sure of that."

"The deaf woman?"

"Gone home to Toronto."

"Capone?"

"Left for parts unknown. I paid him handsomely to let our man leave The Outfit … alive."

"So this Irish thug has no woman and no job. You've done well."

"Thank you, sir."

Andrews got up from his desk and walked to the window. The other man towered over him. The taller man's height and his dark attitude made him intimidating.

"How soon can you bring him around so we can discuss his future, however short we know it to be."

Stratford looked down at his employer. "I'll have him here tomorrow. You just have everything ready, including your daughter."

With that, he turned from the window, strode around the desk to the massive office door, yanked it open and left, leaving the architect relieved and perspiring profusely. If their plan worked, his firm would submit drawings for a new capitol in North Dakota, a beautiful domed showpiece that would be an example to other states and counties throughout the middle of America. This one structure would save his firm from financial ruin and keep him busy for the rest of his lifetime.

He needed to stay busy. Idle time in Ireland had nearly driven him mad. The work had dried up in the south of Ireland, and no British company would hire a Scotch-Irish architect, even though the British had forced his ancestors from Scotland to live among the Catholics in Ireland.

After months of rejections by firm after firm in Dublin and London, and with taxes on his estate escalating, he decided to sell the house and lands to a British overlord and move to America.

He and his wife, Colleen, had discussed the move for months. At night, alone in bed, she had comforted him in his dejections. Each morning she had encouraged him to try again, harder. Finally, when she could no longer summon the strength to encourage him, she said, "We'll move to America."

At the dinner table the next evening, they told Brigid their decision.

"America!!!," she screamed, spitting her food and throwing her fork across the room. "I won't have any friends in bloody America. They're all here."

She got up so fast that she tipped her chair over. She had to jump over it when she stomped from the dining room. "What about my horse?" she yelled. She would never see it again.

-12-

Dó Déag

The following day, O'Connor went to the stockyards. When he reported to the pit boss at his particular livestock pens, the man, a short Jew with a braided graying beard and a jagged scar that ran from the top of his head down to his chin, looked him in the eye.

"Where the fock were you yesterday?"

"Sick."

"Well, Mr. Irish, that there cost you your job, so get the fock away from here!"

O'Connor was stunned. He had always shown up on time, worked hard, and never missed any other days.

"What about my pay?"

"There's no pay for slackards."

O'Connor lunged over the podium and grabbed the pit boss's jacket collar. Just then, two much larger men, the pit boss's constant companions he counted on to quell disturbances over pay, both of whom were bald and had noses spread across their heavily scarred faces from numerous breakings, rushed over, grabbed O'Connor's arms with their strong, unyielding hands, and dragged him backward on his heels.

O'Connor struggled for a few seconds, then pulled his feet under him.

"Let me go," he yelled. "I'll leave on me own!"

The men let go of his arms, and as O'Connor walked

toward the gate, he heard one of the men say in his Wop accent, "Fuckin' goddamn Mick."

O'Connor stopped walking, paused, and then decided to ignore him, for which the man would have been grateful had he known O'Connor at all.

The walk back to the boarding house took O'Connor nearly twice as long as usual. He turned around several times to head back to the stockyards and start a Donnybrook so he could knock some heads, then he thought better about it. Often he sat on a stoop to think about what he would do without a job. Well at least, he thought as he approached the boarding house, I have a place to lay me head while I come up with a plan.

When O'Connor started up the stairs to the boarding house, he looked up to see Mrs. Mickleson's wide hips spanning the open front doorway.

"You're not welcome here no more, O'Connor."

"Move aside woman," O'Connor said standing in front of her now, "I paid 'til the end of next week."

"I'm keeping your money for my shame!"

She stood her ground, her flabby arms crossed over her massive torso.

"I heard what you done to that poor deaf girl you used to bring 'round here. Got her pregnant then beat her so bad she lost the baby."

"I did no such thing!"

"Liar," she screeched. "Two well-dressed men told me just this morning what you done. Now get the hell away from my house," she yelled. "I've already called the coppers."

O'Connor started to argue, but suddenly realized what was happening. Someone wanted him out of town. He didn't know why, but Mary disappearing, losing his jobs, and now his place to stay, were not coincidences.

"I need me grip."

She reached behind her and threw his suitcase at him.

He caught it, then turned and walked slowly down the steps, not knowing what to do next.

As he walked along the street away from the stockyards, he tried to think who could have turned his life upside down and why. He had been through too much to let this turn of circumstances ruin him, but with little money and no place to stay, he would need to think of something soon.

After walking two blocks, O'Connor crossed a street and in the reflection of a shop window, he saw a young boy running at him. O'Connor turned around and the scrawny kid stopped a few feet away, panting and out of breath. He shoved the envelope in his filthy, gray hand at O'Connor.

"You're 'sposed ta read this," he panted. O'Connor tried to grab the kid's hand when he grabbed at the envelope, but the kid had let go of the envelope, making O'Connor catch it in the air with his free hand. When he looked up, the kid had vanished.

Inside the envelope was a piece of embossed note paper on which was typed –

> Suite 1401, Chicago Mercantile Exchange.
> 5:30 this afternoon.
> It was signed simply ~ CA.

O'Connor spent the rest of the day walking the beaches of Lake Michigan. The waves lapping ashore reminded him of harbors in Ireland where the sea had been calmed as it moved inland. He missed Ireland now more than ever. Waves of loneliness and despair swept over him as he contemplated his life, the tragedies, the prejudice, the killing, the war, each one a separate wave of raw grief and deep remorse.

As the sun set and the air cooled, the part inside him that had allowed him to fight and kill when he had to, kicked in. Without noticing, he had walked into the water and his legs were soaked to the knees. He turned and walked now with purpose toward the dry sand. Some people stared at him as if he was out of his mind. When he walked through their midst toward downtown, they averted their eyes. Perhaps I am crazy, he thought. Life's shit certainly makes everyone a little insane.

When O'Connor arrived at the Chicago Mercantile, his pants were dry, and his small suitcase felt like an anvil. He pushed open the brass door and headed toward the bank of lifts. A middle-aged elevator operator, dressed in a uniform with gray pants that had a red stripe on the outside seams, a matching red tunic, and round red cap cocked to one side, held open the elevator doors. Without a word, he closed the doors and moved the brass-handled lever to 14.

They rode up in silence, neither man caring enough to banter about the weather. When the doors opened onto the fourteenth floor, there stood the tall man dressed all in black.

"Mr. O'Connor," he said, "it's good that you're punctual."

"Who the fock are you?"

"I've been watching you for a very long time, Mr. O'Connor," the man said with a raspy, unmistakable British accent. "You were just a lad …"

O'Connor's mind flashed back to the horrific night in Dublin nearly 15 years ago. The gunfire had been chaotic and the failed ambush turned into a massacre. He was running away from the blood when he ran into the tall man, who now stood in front of him. Quickly he processed the face, the callow sneer, the slick backed hair, gray now, but there was no mistaking him.

"And you were a fockin' Brit copper," O'Connor said through clenched teeth. "You bastard!" O'Connor swung at the man, who adroitly sidestepped O'Connor's practiced blow.

Just then the two men who had hauled O'Connor away from the stockyards, grabbed O'Connor's arms. This time, though, O'Connor slipped their grasp and with a knuckle blow to the largest man's Adam's apple, sent him backward, retching and clawing at his own throat. The other man fared worse as O'Connor adroitly ducked from a roundhouse swing and kicked him in the side of his leading knee, the one that bore most of the his weight. As he was going down, O'Connor hit him in the temple with the fury of a wounded bull. The man collapsed. Dead.

"That's quite enough, Mr. O'Connor," the tall man said. He was pointing a Webley Mk IV revolver at O'Connor's head. "I'm quite good with this, especially at such a close range."

O'Connor's clenched fists telegraphed his intention to attack and risk a fatal shot. Just then, another voice, this one with an Irish accent, called out to O'Connor from across the hall.

"Wonderful to see you again, Jack, but don't make me wish I hadn't saved you," the voice said. O'Connor relaxed his fists. The voice was familiar, too familiar. It took him back to Easter Friday 1916, after he had run and run until his lungs burst, until he got away from the Brit murderers who had chased him. This man's foot had nudged him awake; had put him on his horse and taken him home; had the bullet removed then nursed him to health; had allowed him to read books with his daughter. All this and more flashed through O'Connor's mind as he stared at two men he hadn't seen in 15 years. One he hated because of his cruelty, the other he cared for because of his kindness. And here they both were, together in the hall of a skyscraper nearly 3,700 miles from where he'd met them.

"Come in, Lad," the gentler man said, motioning to the office door. "We want to talk a bit."

"If you're with him," O'Connor said pointing to the former British policeman, "then fock off."

"Please, just come in," Clayton Andrews said quietly.

O'Connor stood silently for a minute, unsure what to do, but figured whatever they wanted with him would be better than his current prospects. So he brushed past the two of them and entered the office.

The older man closed the door behind them and looked at O'Connor. "We have a business proposition, Jack."

-13-

TRÍ ÐHÉAG

The gin joint, located in a nondescript alleyway off Rush Street in downtown Chicago, had been decked out by its owner to resemble his favorite pub in Cahir, Ireland, his hometown. Bailey's was always crowded with working stiffs, a few sailors, even a few policemen in uniform.

O'Connor quickly walked down the sidewalk passed Bailey's front door toward the alley. At the mouth of the alley he paused for a moment and glanced up and down the street. Three drunks stumbled out of Bailey's singing a garbled shanty and headed in the opposite direction of the alley. Satisfied that no one appeared to be following him, O'Connor slipped into the alley and strode to the massive sheet metal-clad door barely visible in the dark. Looking around again, he knocked on the door twice, waited a two-count, then knocked four more times. The door swung into the room without as much as a squeak. O'Connor entered quickly, pushed past the bouncer, a short, muscular bald Chinaman with one eye and a cauliflower ear, and began to nudge his way through the crowd and up to the bar.

Once at the bar, O'Connor surveyed the crowd in the mirror over the bar. A burly redheaded bartender, his face, arms and hands covered in faded Celtic warrior tattoos, came over. O'Connor leaned across the bar and said something only the bartender could hear.

The bartender shouted over the din to the Chinaman,

who stood menacingly behind O'Connor.

"Booth by the darts."

With the Chinaman leading the way, the pair jostled through the crowd to a dimly lit booth. Jasper Stratford sat alone drinking a pint of Guinness. O'Connor stood at the table, reached into his pocket and placed a brown piece of paper on the table. Stratford took a sip of his beer and, without looking at O'Connor, picked up the paper and read it. He folded the paper, slipped it into an inside coat pocket, slid out of the booth, picked up his hat and motioned for O'Connor to follow him.

The two men wove their way through the crowd to a back exit. Stratford pulled a wad of money out of his pocket and gave a crisp twenty-dollar bill to the Chinaman, who had anticipated which way Stratford and O'Connor would leave. As he opened the door into a back alley he smiled, showing off a lone gold incisor on an otherwise toothless bottom gum.

Stratford walked nonchalantly 50 yards down the alley as if it was a hall in his home. O'Connor glanced around nervously and followed him. At a corner in the alley they turned into a dead end. Stratford walked up to the shorter alley's lone door, produced a large skeleton key, unlocked it and motioned for O'Connor to enter. O'Connor shook his head no and pulled out his knife. Smiling down at the knife, Stratford turned and crossed the threshold. A light came on.

The room was obviously in a warehouse. It was designed to double as a storeroom and secret conference room or quick escape route from a raid on Bailey's by the Feds.

Wooden crates were stacked on both sides of a narrow path. The smell of fresh vegetables competed with the sweet aroma of oranges and apples. Stratford looked around and found several crates of apples stacked to one side of the path. He motioned to O'Connor to sit.

O'Connor scanned his surroundings, taking stock of nooks where danger might lurk. His instinct and training told him to stay alert.

"Put away the knife, Mr. O'Connor."

"When we're through."

Unaccustomed to his orders being challenged, Stratford's temper rose swiftly. "Then I'm afraid we're finished right now." He rose from the crate.

O'Connor hesitated and then put the knife back in the sheath inside his shirt.

"There's a good fellow. Now Mr. O'Connor, I understand Clayton Andrews has consigned your services for a certain task in North Dakota."

O'Connor stared at him.

"Don't look so surprised. The slaughter houses are unpleasant at best, and a man will do or say almost anything to get out of them. Am I right?"

"What makes you think I know anything about this Bismarck?"

Stratford smiled slyly. "Thank you for confirming my information, Mr. O'Connor. It's good to know that my source is reliable."

O'Connor was stunned. "How ...?"

"I didn't say anything about Bismarck, but you just did. Now, Andrews has some delusion about saving his architectural firm by having you burn down the capitol of North Dakota, right?"

O'Connor stared at Stratford, trying to intimidate him.

"I also happen to know you're a farmer at heart and that you have a certain amount of, um, shall we say 'disdain' for the British and how they treat poor Irish farmers."

O'Connor turned to go. He started to open the door, but Stratford, quick for a large man, jumped up and put his hand on the door. He then grabbed O'Connor and threw him up against the door with a force that stunned the former soldier.

Angry now, Stratford's voice came from deep in his throat. "Now listen to me, potato head. I'm going to make you rich enough to run that beautiful farm of yours and never have to worry about British faggots again, but you've got to trust me."

Stratford let go of O'Connor's lapels, stepped back to the apple crate and sat down. O'Connor straightened his coat and regained his composure.

"And what would YOU be wantin' me to burn down?"

"You make sure that capital building burns to the ground and I'll have the deed to your da's farm in your name when you get back to Ireland."

"What's the rub?"

Stratford handed O'Connor a small card.

"You get your sorry arse back to LaSalle Station downtown, ring up this number. We'll take care of the rest."

"If I don't call?"

"Then some day, Mick, long before the good Lord thought he'd see Jack O'Connor, you'll briefly feel the pain of a razor sliding across your throat."

I ain't no double crosser."

"No, you're a dumb Mick who swings a large hammer against the heads of dumb animals twelve hours a day. And you're about to become an arsonist. If you do that right, you'll make history and no one will ever know your name. Oh, and Andrews will make sure that you'll die before you get out of Dakota."

"Andrews promised me safe passage to Canada and then home," O'Connor said.

"In 1918, a moderately wealthy Clayton Andrews, loyal to the Crown, left Ireland with his wife and young daughter. Some months later, he started an architectural firm right here in downtown Chicago. I believe you've been there, O'Connor."

"Andrews! A BRIT sympathizer??!! That bastard!" O'Connor fumed.

"Still trust him?"

"No, but I'll kill him. The BLOODY barstard!"

"Calm yerself. Just take his money, take our offer and live out your life in quiet bliss."

"How do I know I can trust you?"

"You don't, Boyo. But at least I'm Irish."

"Now there's a guarantee of trustworthiness," O'Connor said sarcastically.

"Just do the job Andrews hired you to do."

O'Connor squared his shoulders, turned full circle, and ran his hands through his hair.

"All right, then. It's a deal. I'll ring the number from the train station as soon as I get back. How do I contact you?"

Stratford got up from the crate and faced O'Connor. "You don't. We'll take care of everything," he said.

"I'm curious," O'Connor said. What exactly do you get out of it?"

"One more of my competitors goes under and I get to design a grand state capitol with a beautiful dome, the likes of which no one has ever seen."

Stratford reached up and turned off the bare bulb light. He and O'Connor felt their way toward the door along the narrow aisle between the crates. Stratford opened the door, looked up and down the alley and motioned for O'Connor to leave.

"Watch your back, Mick" he whispered loudly.

O'Connor smirked and walked down and out of the alley. Stratford turned and locked the door. "That'll make two of us watching your back, Jack O'Connor," Stratford said quietly. Stratford waited a few seconds and walked back to Bailey's.

-14-

ceAtḣAiR óéAg

Bismarck, North Dakota
11:09 p.m., December 27, 1930

O'Connor slept soundly on the dirt floor of the earth lodge, head down, chin resting on his chest, his breath barely visible.

As if on cue he awakened with a start. He opened his eyes wide, reached up and rubbed his scarred hands on his face. He blew into his hands to warm them, sat up, and rotated his head and neck to get the kinks out. He wore a fur hat with long ear flaps, a long buffalo hide coat, heavy breeches, and hobnail boots that he had waterproofed with bear fat.

Sitting in the still of the night, O'Connor thought about what had brought him to this godforsaken place.

The day after his meeting with Stratford, who had given him $1,000 for expenses with the admonition to not "blow" the money on booze and hookers, O'Connor had wandered the streets of Chicago thinking about what he had been hired to do. He vacillated between taking his expense money and heading south or burning down a building in a place he had never heard of. He walked most of the night and shortly before dawn made his way to Union Station where he bought a one-way ticket to Bismarck.

"What's in Bismarck for ya," the ticket agent asked, smiling as he took O'Connor's money. O'Connor didn't answer. He preferred to not concoct some fictional reason for his travels.

As the ticket agent pushed the ticket and change to O'Connor, his expression flattened. "Ain't much of a town," he said. "Probably won't find a job there."

O'Connor scooped up the ticket and his change. "Thanks for the advice," he said, glaring into the agent's eyes before walking away.

"At least you'll be warm in that coat," the agent said to O'Connor's back.

He had bought the full-length buffalo coat from an old Indian who approached him as the old man shuffled out of Saint Nicholas Mission in Chicago. The old man had looked pleadingly at him through eye slits narrowed by years in the sun, so, knowing winter was fast approaching, O'Connor paid 20 dollars for the coat. The man had shaken his hand vigorously and shuffled back into the mission, presumably to get a free meal. What O'Connor didn't see was the old man's grin as he straightened up and counted his money several times.

When he boarded the westbound train headed toward Bismarck with long scheduled stops at St. Paul, Minnesota, and Fargo, North Dakota, and whistle stops at virtually every town in between, O'Connor felt all eyes on him as he made his way through the passenger cars until he found a seat near a window where he could stretch his legs without some eejit stumbling over them to take a piss.

His seat was plush and comfortable. The train company had recently renovated older cars and bought new cars designed to attract passengers and to stave off competition from the emerging airlines. As soon as O'Connor settled in, he covered himself with the buffalo coat and was rocked to sleep soon after the train left Chicago.

The clackity-clack of the train wheels invaded his dreams and brought him back to riding the train out of the war zone to the coast of France. He began to mumble in his sleep, but remained asleep even when other passengers frightened by his jabbering, moved out of earshot. Soon O'Connor had the front of the car all to himself. He slept most of the ride to St. Paul, waking momentarily whenever the train pulled into some small snow-covered berg along the tracks.

When the train finally arrived in Fargo, North Dakota, for a four-hour stop to change the crew and offload freight, O'Connor put his small bag on his seat to reserve it, threw on his coat, and disembarked. As he stepped onto the platform and into the frigid air that took away his breath, he saw a station agent flapping his arms to stay warm.

"Where can I get a bite?" O'Connor asked him.

"Can't," he replied, his breath frozen in the air. "Everything's closed. It's Sunday."

"Damn!"

"But we got sandwiches and hot coffee in the station," the station agent said.

"Why didn't you tell me first off?"

"Thought they told you on the train," he replied. "Six bucks."

"Six bucks," O'Connor exclaimed. "You're daft!" He returned to the train, boarded and returned to his seat, mumbling "six bucks" the entire way.

The train stopped again in Valley City and Jamestown, where O'Connor was able to get off during the 60 minute stop and find a café where he got a full dinner of stringy roast beef, lumpy mashed potatoes, and soggy green peas, with coffee for $2.50. "Six bucks!" the manager heard him say as he left the eatery.

O'Connor stayed awake the rest of the trip across the most desolate land he had ever seen. Watching the snow-covered prairie stream by made him even more determined to return to the lush green landscape of Ireland. But to get there required perfect execution of the plan he had devised. Now he needed to review his plan. Again.

The glare off the snow forced O'Connor to avert his eyes from the boring scenery. He closed them to calm the nerves that started to jitter whenever he contemplated his task.

Stratford had given him a newspaper article that reported on the recent erection of a replica of an Indian dwelling just to the east of the North Dakota capital building. O'Connor noted its location relative to the building and began to formulate his plan of attack. First, the Indian mound would provide the perfect hiding place in the early evening. He would then make his way from it to the building in the dead of night.

Stratford had made sure he had the right incendiary for his task, and O'Connor's small burlap travel bag held a flask of naphtha.

Stratford guaranteed transportation away from the capitol. He had told O'Connor to head north where he would find a truck that had been overhauled and fitted with an extra gas tank for the long trip to Jamestown, 100 miles east.

If he worked the plan, everything would go as expected, O'Connor told himself. Just work the bloody plan.

After getting off the train in Bismarck that afternoon, O'Connor had walked the city's downtown streets, burlap bag slung over his shoulder. Anyone who saw him would think he was just another homeless bum in search of work. His buffalo coat might make someone look twice, but his phony downtrodden look and downcast eyes would dispel any suspicion.

He didn't eat anywhere because he wanted to maintain the pretence of poverty, nor did he beg for handouts because that might draw attention. He just shuffled along, going over and over his plan. As evening approached, he slowly headed toward the capitol.

It was an ugly brick structure that had served as the Dakota Territory capitol before the territory was divided on November 2, 1889, into the new states of North and South Dakota.

Not much else was added to the grounds until 1908 when Theodore Roosevelt's Maltese Cross Cabin was moved from Fargo's State Fair Grounds to the Capitol Grounds.

In the fall of 1929, an Indian Earth Lodge was erected on the Capitol Grounds near Roosevelt's cabin as another way to draw tourists by showing them how Mandan Indians had lived when Lewis and Clark first paddled up to their villages along the Missouri River. It will serve as the perfect hiding place, O'Connor thought.

He had taken his time getting to the capitol grounds. He had even walked around a few blocks until the sky was completely dark before he headed into the earth lodge. Now, after a few hours of fitful sleep, O'Connor stood up, stretched his back, moved his feet and legs to warm and limber them up. He reached into the right coat pocket, pulled out a piece of jerked meat and slowly chewed it while listening for any sounds outside.

Still chewing, O'Connor reached down and picked up the burlap bag at his feet. There was a soft clink from inside the bag.

Holding the bag tightly against his chest, he walked to the entrance of the round earth lodge. He glanced outside, and seeing only the moon glistening off the snowy grounds, came back inside, reached overhead to one of the log cross beams, and pulled down the pine bough he had placed there earlier. He walked over to where he had been sleeping and methodically swept the pine bough over the dirt floor.

Stepping back, he inspected his work. Satisfied that no one would be able to tell he had spent the last few hours there, he backed out of the lodge, brushing away his tracks as he went. He stopped at the entrance, turned and peered outside. Seeing nothing suspicious, he bent over and shuttled away from the lodge, brushing his tracks in the dirt. He could see other footprints in the lodge, but he ignored them.

At 29 years old, O'Connor had been hardened by war and by twelve years of bare-knuckle boxing in Ireland and America. The training, running seven or eight miles every day while carrying 10-pound weights in each hand, had been almost as brutal as the actual boxing matches.

Fighting in the ring and in back alleys had, however, kept him in top shape for his job as mob enforcer in New York and Chicago. Those connections and his reputation for leaving no traces that would betray him or his bosses had earned him the job of burning down the North Dakota capital building.

O'Connor arched his back against the slanted side of the dirt lodge so he was almost invisible. The crisp night air was clear, the stars blinked at O'Connor. The full moon illuminated the sky and the snow-covered landscape of the expansive Capitol Grounds, which would cause him to cast a shadow on his approach.

"Damn!" He swore under his breath.

Careful to walk in other tracks around the lodge, he edged his way around, his back still hugging the lodge.

As he moved, two large buildings came into view. O'Connor searched the moonlit ground and found what he was looking for – a worn path in the snow heading in the direction of the buildings. He had spied it the previous afternoon when he scouted the place.

Holding tightly to the burlap bag with his right hand, the pine bough in the other, O'Connor hunched his back, bent his knees, and trotted toward the buildings.

He stayed on the path that ran between the two buildings until he reached a small evergreen beside it. He paused, lifted his leg and held it for a few seconds. He turned back to the tree trunk, stuck his head close to it, and pretended to sniff for a few seconds. He hunched over and ran to the larger building. Anyone seeing him would just think he was a large stray dog.

When he reached the door at the side of the large, red-brick building, he straightened up, looked left then right, gently slid the bag to the ground, reached into his pocket and pulled out a key.

O'Connor's timing was perfect. Before he unlocked the door he had watched and waited until the night watchman reached the furthest point on the top floor in his rounds.

He slowly looked around again, put the key in the door, and turned it and the door knob simultaneously. The door opened. He smiled slightly, looked over both shoulders, and gently picked up the burlap bag. He slid through the narrow opening, still holding the pine bough, and closed the door with his back.

Even though O'Connor placed his feet silently, his

hobnail boots still clomped like gunshots on the wood floor as he started to walk down the long main floor hall. He stopped, removed them, and carried them in his free hand.

Moonlight streamed through tall windows at the ceiling. That light illuminated his face until he was midway down the hall. Then he was in darkness. He walked to a door in the middle of the wall and set down his burlap bag and the pine bough. Looking around, he smiled. There were no other sounds as he opened the well-oiled closet door.

He sniffed two or three times inside the closet, reached down and picked up the pine bough, which he laid over a pile of oily rags at the back of the closet.

Reaching back behind his right foot, he pulled the burlap bag in front of him, opened it, reached in and pulled out two silver flasks, which he gently placed on the closet floor. Then he laid the burlap bag on the pine bough.

O'Connor paused again to listen. He drew his killing knife from its sheath strapped to his waist and chopped holes in the back and side walls of the closet. When he was satisfied with the size of the holes, he uncorked the flask filled with naphtha and poured the contents over the pile in front of him. The liquid glugged over the rags. Just for good measure, he poured a mixture of linseed oil and naphtha from the other flask into the holes on the walls.

Stepping back from the closet, he surveyed his handiwork briefly, pulled a match out of his shirt pocket, and struck it on the door jam. The flaring match illuminated his face just before he threw it on the rags.

The flash made him reel backward slightly. The pile burned quickly as the accelerant ignited producing a temperature high enough to light the oil. When flames began to lick the clapboard closet walls and smoke vented up through the holes he had chopped into them, the arsonist stood transfixed. Sweat beaded on his face, the blaze reflected in his eyes.

-15-

CÚIG DÉAG

The flames shone bright on O'Connor's face; the heat brought him out of his trance. He shook his head, and looked to the top of the closet. Seeing that the flames had broken through the ceiling, he quickly stepped into the hall and swung the closet door almost closed, leaving it open a crack to give the fire air. He turned and headed back down the hall toward his point of entry. His stocking feet padded across the wood floor, barely audible over the sound of muffled crackling flames.

At the stairwell, he looked back and watched the glow shining beneath the closet door before bolting down the stairs. On the ground floor he walked to the door he'd entered and pulled on his boots and quickly tied the laces.

Once outside, O'Connor hugged the building as he inched his way toward his escape route. At the sound of voices he froze. He pulled the key out of his pocket, slid back to the door, and inserted the key into the lock. It refused to turn. The voices came closer, grew louder.

A man said, "C'mon, Edna. We'll snuggle over here."

"Eli Burke, you take me home this instant. I've had too much of Granny Burke's Christmas nog," a woman laughed.

The man pushed a canning jar at her. "Just one more drink, Edna. It's good for what ails ya."

Flattened against the portico of the entry, O'Connor slowed his breathing. He took deep breaths through his mouth, exhaled slowly through his nose so his breath would not give him away.

As the couple got closer, O'Connor reached under his coat and drew his knife. He had carried it through the war and through the streets of New York City and Chicago. O'Connor preferred the 10-inch blade to a gun because, honed to razor-like sharpness, the weapon was silent, deadly and personal, which was important. The men he had killed were either enemy soldiers or deserved to die for some other reason. These two didn't deserve to die, but he could not risk being discovered. In an instant he decided he would place their bodies in a lovers' pose at the inside corner next to the entrance.

Before that became necessary, the young woman slipped and fell in the snow at the corner of the building closest to O'Connor's hiding spot. Neither she nor Eli sensed anything or saw anything but one another.

"Wheee," she giggled. Half lying down, she stayed for a few seconds in the snow. "Now I've done it, Eli. I'm wet and it's very cold. Please take me home."

"Oh, all right, darling."

Eli clumsily reached down, grabbed her under her armpits, and hauled her upright. They turned and stumbled their way through the snow, heading for the lighted neighborhood across the street from the capital building. O'Connor watched them go. He lifted his right hand, wiped away a sweat rivulet between his temple and chiseled jawline, and sheathed his knife.

When Edna and Eli were almost to the street, O'Connor hunched down and ran in a weaving pattern perpendicular to their path. When he reached a small bush, he paused, lifted one leg, held it up for a few seconds, and then moved a few feet away stopping next to a wood post holding a wooden sign. He turned, looked back at Edna and Eli stumbling up the steps of a small house. Behind them lay the sleeping town of Bismarck.

O'Connor slowly surveyed the scene. A trolley car parked by the building, its tracks running past the other large building and down through a residential area into the town's business district. Just east of the second large building sat a log cabin surrounded by a low picket fence. At the southeast corner of the large area south of the log cabin stood the recreated Mandan Indian earth lodge where he had spent the hours before doing visiting the capitol.

Shaking his head at the beauty of the peaceful scene, O'Connor turned and loped away. Glancing backward at the sign that was atop the wooden post where he'd paused. Its words were barely visible in the moonlight: "North Dakota Capitol".

Still walking hunched over, O'Connor approached a small flatbed truck. He opened the driver's side door, reached in, adjusted the throttle, went around the open door and turned the crank at the front of the truck. Nothing. He cranked several more times, stopped, looked around, listened. Silence. Moonlight glistened off the snow on the ground and the roofs of the houses. Slivers of smoke rose from chimneys that jutted into the night. Flames licked at the windows of the capitol.

O'Connor went again to the driver's side, reached in, pulled the choke out of the firewall, went back to the front of the truck and turned the crank. This time the engine caught and sputtered to life. He ran back, reached in and pushed the choke half way in. As the engine picked up speed, he pushed in the choke more. The engine began to run smoothly so he pushed the choke in most of the way, and waited.

Back in the distance, a red glow was visible from the top floor of the North Dakota Capitol. O'Connor tapped his fingers on the steering wheel. He pushed the choke in all the way and the engine settled into a smooth putter. He went to the front of the truck and pulled out the crank lever.

Back in the cab, O'Connor took a breath, adjusted the throttle again, pushed the clutch to the floorboard, shifted into first gear and drove off.

~16~
SÉ DÉAG

Eli and Edna stumbled up the steps to the house. Eli tripped on the middle step and fell upward, banging hard on the porch.

"Sshhh. You'll wake my parents!"

"Sssshhhh," Eli slurred.

"I'm going in to bed. You go home, Eli!"

"I'm going home. You go to bed."

"'That's what I just said," she giggled.

Eli struggled to his feet and put his left hand on the storm door. As he leaned down, Edna raised her face to meet his kiss. Their lips parted and her tongue met his as he explored the inside of her upper lip. He brought his right hand up under her coat and caressed her breast. She let him keep his hand on her breast until he began to press his thumb into her nipple.

"Not now and especially not here, Eli." She twisted away and yanked open the storm door. As quietly as she could, she unlocked the front door and went inside. Before Eli turned away, Edna drew aside the lace curtain covering the door's window and peeked out. She loved him even though he was a high school English teacher and not a doctor like her mother thought she should find. But she couldn't help how she felt about him.

Outside, Eli leaned his head against the door jam and gently placed the palm of his right hand on the window.

"Good night, sweet Juliet."

Eli turned on his heels and stumbled down the steps almost falling. Straightening up, he walked south on the gravel street, which was covered with snow-packed ice.

He half slid a short distance before he turned onto a wood walkway leading to the boarding house he shared with five other single men. Eli stumbled up the steps and fell into a swing on the front porch. Lifting his head, he looked at the Capitol across the street. He blinked his eyes several times. They refused to focus. Besides that, he couldn't believe what he thought he saw.

Eli shook his head to clear his brain. He still wasn't sure, but he could swear he saw lights shining in the building. He narrowed his eyelids, trying to focus.

"Fire," he croaked.

He chewed his tongue a few times, swallowed and tried to focus his eyes. He cleared his throat and yelled.

"My God! It's on FIRE!"

He tried to get out of the swing. It slipped out from underneath him and he sprawled on the porch.

"FIRE! THE CAPITOL'S ON FIRE!" he shouted as he scrambled to get up, and promptly vomited.

Adrenalin had sobered him up somewhat and he ran down the steps to the middle of the gravel street. Standing in the middle of the street, looking at the Capitol, he yelled until he thought his throat would bleed.

"The Capitol's on fire. Fire! Fire! It's on fire. The Capitol. Fire."

Lights came on in a few houses along the street. Several voices yelled, "Shut up!"

In the firehouse a mile south of the burning capitol, three firemen snored in the quiet Bismarck night. Downtown was dark, save for three street lights spaced two blocks apart. A few shops had Christmas wreathes hanging on their doors, which were illuminated by the moonlight streaming through the buildings.

Somewhere a phone rang. Elmer Black rolled over and jammed the pillow over his head. Answer that damnable phone, he thought.

Finally he realized the ringing was coming from across the room. He rolled out of the rickety metal-framed bed, shuffled sleepily to the crank phone on the wall, stuffed his left index finger into his left ear and put the earpiece to his right ear.

"Yah, what is it?"

He listened for a few seconds, trying to hear the voice on the other end of the phone.

"Slow down, Ethyl. Don't go getting your bloomers in a bind. What about the Capitol?"

He listened a few more seconds, holding the earpiece away from his ear to spare his hearing from the voice screaming at him. He slammed the earpiece into the hanger and, reaching to the wall, he flipped a switch.

"Get up, boys. We got us a live one!"

The clang from the brass fire bell startled the other two firemen awake. They swung out of bed. Adrenaline flowing through them like melted snow through a swollen creek in springtime, they pulled on their canvas pants and large leather boots, pushed arms through suspenders as they ran to the corner of the dormitory bedroom and slid down the pole into the garage through the hole in the floor.

One fireman slid behind the wheel of the 1925 Federal Knight Fire truck. The other man jumped into the Ahrens Fox. The engines started immediately and ran smoothly.

Black pushed open the large doors, ran back between the two trucks, and jumped on the side of the Ahrens Fox. As he climbed aboard he yelled to the drivers.

"The State Capitol!"

The men looked at him, wide-eyed, stunned.

"Go! GO! GO!"

The Ahrens Fox pulled out of the garage followed by the Federal Knight. Black immediately grabbed the rope attached to the bell and pulled. The other driver reached above his head and turned the siren crank. Both trucks raced north on Fourth Street where they could see the glow against the winter night sky.

A small crowd of people dressed in pajamas and winter coats had gathered on the circular road that approached the Capitol. They all turned in unison to watch as the two fire trucks, bells clanging and sirens blaring, roared up. The firemen jumped out, assembled their equipment and ran to douse the blaze, which had reached the top floors.

The firemen slipped and slid in the snow toward the Capitol, dragging the stiff hoses behind them. A few of the men in the crowd, dressed only in pajamas and coats, ran to help them. Black turned valves on each truck. Water dribbled out of the hoses. Stunned, both firemen banged the brass nozzles on the ground. The water trickled out.

The crowd watched the blaze completely engulf the Capitol and light up the pre-dawn sky. Many of the crowd drank coffee while some held children and pointed to the burning building. A man drove up in a car with the name "Finney's" lettered in gold on the door, got out, stared at the scene and then got back in his car. A few minutes later, he emerged with a large camera and tripod. He set up the rig and ducked under the black fabric shade on the camera back.

More spectators drove up and parked their cars on the mall. A man and a woman climbed through a ground-floor window in the capital building, only to race out a few minutes later. The woman held a large book and the man ran a few feet, stumbled and jammed his blistered hands into a snow bank. Close to the burning building, the firemen worked frantically on the fire trucks.

"FROZEN! The idiotic pumps are FROZEN!" Blacked yelled.

He kicked the side of the fire truck. The two other firemen walked back to the trucks, dragging the frozen hoses with them. From behind them an explosion rocked the building and shook the ground. At the sound of the blast all three firemen instinctively ducked and turned.

The crowd oohed and aahed. Some of the children watching the fire clapped at the sounds, others threw snowballs at each other and at the fire.

At the back of the crowd Jasper Stratford surveyed the scene. He was dressed in a long black leather coat with a beaver fur collar and a large matching fur hat. A wool muffler tightly circled his neck. He peered at the fire trucks, at the crowd enjoying the show. Stratford then reached into his pocket and gently drew out a homing pigeon with a bright red band around one leg. He nestled the pigeon near his lips.

"Home!" he whispered.

Stratford threw the pigeon into the air. It fluttered and flew higher to circle the burning building. Once it got it's heading from the sun, it headed east.

Stratford watched. After the bird finally headed east, he walked over to a Model T, casually looked around and opened the passenger door. He unlatched the door on a small cage on the seat, reached into his coat pocket and pulled out another pigeon. This one wore a white band around its leg. Stratford cooed to the pigeon, gently put it in the cage, and closed the cage door. Once the pigeon had settled in, Stratford reached over to the firewall and pulled the car's throttle half way out. He then walked to the front of the car and cranked the handle. The car started immediately, so he pulled out the crank and slowly walked to the driver's side, got in behind the steering wheel. As he adjusted the choke and throttle until the engine purred, he looked out through the windshield at the burning building. Smiling smugly, he turned the steering wheel and did a U-turn. He saw the burning building in the reflection of his windshield. When the pigeon arrived in Chicago, his head team of architects would begin the final designs on North Dakota's new capitol.

-17-

seacht déag

Fifty-three miles East of Bismarck, North Dakota
December 28, 1930

Stratford's pigeon flew low so she could easily spot any place that might shelter her from the wind and cold. Flying low also let her spot grain spills on the gravel roads that crisscrossed the frozen prairie. These were dangerous but critical respites.

In the winter on the prairie every animal was a potential meal for raptors. Falcons and hawks were always on the lookout, although because of her speed and experience, the little pigeon might prove too much work for a bird of prey. A raptor would break off the chase of a bird because it was consuming too much precious energy. A rabbit or ground squirrel caught unaware was easier to catch.

Hungry and in need of rest, the pigeon flew low over a gas station at the side of a country road. She knew that grain and gravel could be available near the station.

Below her, a man dressed in striped grey coveralls and a dirty winter coat stood in the front room of the small building. He looked out a dusty window to the west. As he began to turn away, he saw a small flatbed truck coming over the hill toward the station. He pulled a revolver up to his face, opened the back and slowly spun the cylinder. He put the gun on the window sill.

A pregnant woman waddled out of the outhouse behind the gas station. She leaned against the outhouse door and put her hand on her stomach. Swallowing back nausea, she pushed herself off the door and shuffled toward the back door of the gas station.

From the corner of her eye she saw the roadster parked under a clump of trees up the road from the station. Strange, she thought.

Hilda slowly pushed open the back door and saw her husband, Hans, gagged and tied to a straight-back chair. He had a purple gash on his forehead and blood ran from his nose toward his mouth. She opened her mouth to speak and he shook his head "No". She rushed over to untie him.

At the same time the truck pulled up to the lone gasoline pump. O'Connor shut off the engine and rested his head on the steering wheel for a few seconds.

The man peered out the window as the flatbed truck pulled up to the gas pump. When he saw O'Connor put his head on the steering wheel, he reached in his shirt pocket and pulled out a small photo. He studied the photo, looked out the window and back at the photo. Satisfied that this was the Mick the Andrews brothers wanted him to kill, he slipped the photo back into his pocket, picked up the gun and cocked the hammer. He held it behind his back and opened the station's rickety door.

"Howdy. Need gas?"

"Yep. In the reserve tank on the bed, too."

"Got it."

O'Connor walked to the rear of the truck. As he bent down to check the left tire, the killer walked cautiously to the driver's side and raised the pistol.

Just then Hans came around the corner of the small clapboard building pointing an ancient double-barreled shotgun at the killer.

"You freeze right there, Mr.!"

O'Connor froze. Startled, the man with the pistol fired a quick shot, just missing O'Connor and kicking up gravel two inches from his left foot. O'Connor dove behind the tire. The man quickly fired off another shot at O'Connor then swung his gun hand toward Hans.

The shotgun blast took off the left side of the man's head before his arm made the full swing at Hans.

O'Connor crawled out from behind the tire and peered up over the bed of the truck, first at Hans and then at the man sprawled on the ground with half his head missing. Blood seeped into the ground around him.

"Jasus!"

"You okay, Mr.?" asked Hans.

O'Connor, visibly shaken, and Hans walked to the body.

"Bastard comb in here all nice and all. Minute I turned my back, he clobbered me one. I vake up tied to my office chair mit a sore head. He ain't too shmart, though."

"How's that?"

A shaken Hilda brought over a coat and Hans put it on. It had a sheriff's badge on the left breast pocket.

"I been real close to the sheriff," Hans said with a laugh.

"No von messes mit my Hans," Hilda said. "He'ss da Emmins County sherriv."

O'Connor swallowed hard. "What ... what d'ya suppose this arsehole wanted?"

"You a Mick, den?" Hilda scoffed upon hearing O'Connor's brogue.

"Hilda!" Hans scolded her.

O'Connor looked at Hilda. "You a Kraut, DEN?"

Looking down at the body, Hans repeated to O'Connor what had happened hoping to distract Hilda.

"He valks up here, so I tink he runs out of gas. Ve, Hilda und me, ve don't get much traffic on this road so early in the morning. I volk up gagged and tied to my office chair."

As he talked, the sheriff filled both gas tanks on O'Connor's truck ignoring the dead man. The bastard can lay there as long as I gottdamn vell please, he thought as he stepped over the body.

O'Connor had gone inside the little gas station to warm up. The coal stove put out just enough heat to take off the morning chill. The room smelled like burning coal and gasoline.

Hilda stood next to him watching her husband wipe the truck's windshield. She saw the dead man's feet and legs then turned her head to glare at O'Connor. "Beeg coat! Varm?"

O'Connor calmly scanned the scene outside the window. A few war kills flashed through his mind and he forced them away.

"Yah, it's "varm," he mimicked her accent.

Hilda stared into his eyes. She wasn't afraid of no Irish. Probably a Papist, too, she thought. O'Connor stared back. It was a stand-off until Hans walked through the door.

"That'll be fife dollars and tirty-nine cents."

O'Connor reached into his pocket and threw the gold coin on the counter.

"I don't haf change for dat."

"Keep it."

O'Connor walked out the door.

"Feckin' Kraut," he said to himself as he stepped over the body's feet and slid onto the truck seat. O'Connor adjusted the throttle and the choke. He started to get out with the crank and looked up to see Hans standing in front of the truck, staring at him. O'Connor reached under a blanket on the seat next to him and grasped the handle of his knife.

"I'll crank for you," Hans said.

O'Connor slowly withdrew his hand from under the blanket. " Thanks."

Hans came to the driver's window. O'Connor handed him the crank and he inserted it in the engine, turned the crank a couple of times, the truck started, and he handed the crank through the window to O'Connor as he pulled away. He looked in the rear view mirror. Hans and Hilda stood over the body, watching carefully as he drove away, as if they were memorizing everything about his truck.

-18-
OCHT DÉAG

Sixty-seven miles East of Bismarck, North Dakota
December 28, 1930

The woman leaned against the rumble seat trunk of the yellow and black Model-A Roadster. She had removed the spare tire and placed it beside the left rear fender. She waited patiently, but her feet were getting cold and she hated having cold feet.

Attractive with flaming red hair surrounding an angular face adorned with perfectly placed freckles on alabaster skin, she wore her favorite black riding pants, black riding boots, and a fur-trimmed tan leather jacket. She looked like she was driving to her father's riding stables instead of driving across North Dakota in December.

Brigid Elizabeth Andrews loved her father, which was the only reason she had allowed him to talk her into waiting on the side of the road to kill a man her father wanted dead and who may or may not come, depending on the success or failure of a Chicago mob guy her father had hired to do the job; that and the possibility that her generous allowance would cease if his architectural firm didn't get this new project.

He had raised her alone since two years after they moved to America, as alone as a father can who employs a day nanny and a night nurse to watch over his only child. Brigid fondly remembered her mother, who, had succumbed after the move to laudanum. She had begun taking it to dull her persistent violent headaches and the panic attacks that accompanied them. Eventually the opiate transitioned from helpful pain reliever to debilitating habit. She used it more as a prophylactic than a remedy, to prevent the starbursts and crazies, she told her husband.

When Brigid was seventeen, her father had shipped mums off to a sanitarium, where she was supposed to be weaned off the drug. One night, according to the report in her file, she doubled over and shook so violently that the orderly and two nurses had to move her, in restraints, to a quiet room. Somehow during the short walk she twisted out of their grasp, ran down a corridor, and leaped out a second-floor hall window.

When the staff reached the window scant seconds later, they saw their patient running toward the woods that surrounded the hospital. Although the staff, aided by the Chicago police, looked throughout the night and well into the following afternoon, Colleen Andrews had disappeared and was never seen again. At least that's what Brigid's father had told her whenever she asked about her mother.

Standing in his office with him, Brigid listened intently to her father.

"You, dear girl, will be our safety net. If the Mick somehow gets by our man, it will be up to you to make sure the Irishman doesn't get to Fargo," he had told her as they looked out over the Chicago skyline from his massive office. He wore his signature blue pinstriped suit, starched white shirt with a maroon and blue rep bow tie, gold cufflinks, and black and white patent leather shoes. His salt and pepper hair was slicked back in the current style, and his gold-rimmed eye glasses rested low on the bridge of his nose.

He spoke to his daughter without the slightest hint of malice, more like telling her about a recent company outing to watch the Chicago White Sox play the New York Yankees at Comiskey Park.

"We've been assured by our political operatives in Bismarck that we will get the job to design a new capitol for North Dakota," he continued, never turning to face her, "but first we need to remove the current structure and erase any connection we might have to the, um, unfortunate tragedy."

Clayton Andrews wore his wealth like a badge of honor. Although he had never had to struggle hard since migrating to America from his beloved Ireland, he had invested long hours as an architect designing skyscrapers using the tools and techniques of the early 20th Century. During those long days in the office, his only child lived in a townhouse on Chicago's tony east side, which he had purchased with the proceeds from the sale of his expansive country estate in County Wicklow.

After the stock market crash in 1929, many surviving companies had gotten nervous and had cancelled some projects that were in the planning stages. No governments had gotten nervous. They were still building. And so the firm of Andrews and Andrews had begun courting state and county governments throughout the upper Midwest. Eventually, though, even governments had begun to hold off, requiring enterprising architectural firms to employ ever more creative methods of securing contracts. Bribes, blackmail, and coercion became the norm. Money moved from man to man like drunken hookers at a speakeasy.

Being the only child of a wealthy man, Brigid had had

only the best of everything – the best schools, the best tutors, the best tennis coaches, the best close-combat trainers. Her father had insisted on the latter because, as he told her often, life was cruel and filled with evil men who would take advantage of an attractive woman. Not only must she be a lady, she should be able to kick the stuffings out of any man who tried to hurt her. If he continued, she had learned several ways to stop him. Permanently.

Her skills and training changed her life the night she and three of her sorority sisters had talked their way into a speakeasy at the edge of the bad part of Chicago. On their way back to the campus, her sisters wanted to take a taxi, but Brigid wanted to walk off the Canadian whiskey, so they hailed a taxi and she walked on alone. After walking two blocks, she heard footsteps coming up quickly behind her. Brigid walked faster; the footsteps got louder. Just as she turned to see how close they were, a hand grabbed her arm and swung her all the way around and into the bear hug of a second man. When the first man started to tear off her blouse, Brigid braced herself against the man holding her and kicked out with all her might. The power of her kick stunned the man, giving Brigid enough time to drive the back of her head into the nose of the man holding her. He loosened his grasp and when he did she twisted around in his arms to face him and struck him in the nose with the heel of her hand driving the bridge of his nose into his brain killing him instantly.

Then a blow to her head from behind caused her to nearly pass out, but she didn't wait for a second blow. She twirled around and sweep kicked to where she thought her attacker would be. Thanks to her training she guessed right and her foot connected with the man's knee, dislocating it.

He screamed, "You fucking bitch!" and hobbled forward and tried to grab her around the neck. Brigid used his forward motion to pull his left arm away from her and with a fluid motion twisted it behind his back and slammed his face into the brick wall of the building next to them. Infuriated now, she grabbed the hair on the back of his head and repeatedly bashed his head into the wall until his face was a bloody pulp. When another hand grabbed her arm, Brigid violently whirled around into the arms of a large policeman.

"Whoa, missy," he said. "Stop now!"

Brigid glared at the officer and began to shake, but not from fear. The fight had excited her so much she wanted more of it.

After the bodies were hauled away in a paddy wagon, Officer Patrick O'Bourne had asked her several times to describe what had happened. Her story was the same each time, so he figured she was telling the truth.

"We may hafta call you for a written statement, but I'm familiar with them two and the world is better off without 'em, so I think this is the end of it for you," he had said after writing her name and address in his log book.

Brigid had been so exhilarated that she ran most of the way back to her sorority so she could brag about her prowess. She did, to anyone who would listen. After that night, all her sorority sisters gave her wide berth and for the second time since moving to America, Brigid Andrews had no friends.

"But I don't want to move to America," she had whined to her parents when they told her about their decision. "All my friends are here!"

Her friends all lived in the village. So did her tutors. But the worst thing about moving was leaving her favorite horse behind. She and Red had grown up together. Da and Ma had presented the colt to her on her fourth birthday. His gleaming auburn color earned him the name Red in honor of Erik the Red, the Viking whom Da said raided Ireland and brought some civilization to the wild Celts. Da said all Irish were descended from the Vikings, and that's why they were fighters and drinkers.

Unfortunately, Da designed buildings for a living, and America was where buildings needed to be built, not in Ireland. Besides, Da had dreams of building huge buildings, what they called skyscrapers in America.

Her fierce loyalty to her father and her fierceness in a fight had brought her to the narrow shoulder of a narrow highway on the frigid plains of central North Dakota.

She parked her roadster on the shoulder at the down slope side of a hill. Leaning against the trunk, she was as relaxed as only a self-confident woman can be. Down the hill, she saw the blood-red truck cresting on the far hill. Pushing herself off the trunk with her buttocks, she took a deep breath and quickly went to the passenger side car where she picked up the ice pick she had stuck in the ground. She bent down, swung the pick and easily punctured the gas tank. As fuel began squirting out, she threw the ice pick into the adjacent field, walked to the back of the car, and again leaned against the trunk.

As the truck approached, Brigid nonchalantly pushed herself away from the car and stood in the middle of the road. As the truck approached, she waved her arms over her head and jumped up and down.

O'Connor peered down the road at the car and the figure in the middle of the road. He drove past the woman and stopped a few feet in front of the roadster. Before getting out he slid the knife under his side of the seat. Just as he pulled his arm up, the woman appeared at his window.

"Afternoon!" she said cheerfully. "At least I think it is after noon."

O'Connor glanced up the road. No other cars were on the horizon.

"What's the matter, Lass?"

"Car just sputtered and died. I don't know what's wrong."

O'Connor sized her up. With a quick scan he noted the curve of her jacket, the shape of her lips and her fiery red hair. Attraction sparked deep in his brain. He unconsciously smiled.

"I'll take a look."

Brigid stepped aside so O'Connor could get out of the truck. O'Connor walked to the rear of the roadster. He saw the spare tire and then the faint odor of gasoline reached his nose. He sniffed harder and then spied the wet snow and gravel at the rear of the car.

Brigid followed his gaze.

"Oh, my!"

"Fuel leak."

He got down on his hands and knees to look under the car. Brigid recognized him from the photograph she had in her jacket. She wondered how he had gotten passed the professional killer, but he had, so now saving da was up to her. She reached into her jacket and wrapped her fingers around the .41 caliber pearl-handled derringer.

From under the car, O'Connor said, "Something's punched a hole in your petrol tank."

Brigid started to pull the small gun out of her jacket pocket, but hesitated. In that instant O'Connor stood up and faced her, his face a foot away and he towered over her. The opportunity to put two bullets into the back of his head had escaped. She would have to wait.

"Not much I can do, Lass. You'll be riding with me to the next town, wherever that is in this godforsaken place," he said.

Stepping around him in the snow, Brigid opened the roadster's passenger door, reached in and grabbed a leather duffle bag. As she closed the car's door, O'Connor was already at the truck. She tromped through the snow on the shoulder, opened the door, threw the bag on the truck seat, and jumped in.

"Home, Jeeves!"

O'Connor gave her a quick, easy smile. But as he looked at her, he had the feeling that he had seen her before. There was something familiar about the way she held her head to one side, the freckles that dotted the bridge of her nose, the red-orange hair. Finally, though, he concluded that her familiar appearance was because she looked like half the girls in Ireland. Pushing aside any further thoughts, he shifted into first gear and headed the truck down the center of the road.

-19-

NAOI DÉAG

Speeding and darting through the grey winter sky on the third day of her flight, the young homing pigeon flew over eastern Minnesota's frozen lakes and dormant trees that reached toward the clouds with their naked limbs like condemned souls in a dreary medieval painting pleading Heaven for mercy from the cold.

She had lost weight and needed more frequent rest periods, but she was strong and possessed an infallible sense of direction.

Sensing instinctively that the quiet of this morning meant she needed to be more vigilant, she rose high and flew in a wide arcing circle so she could check for predators. And then the red hawk appeared out of nowhere, its body camouflaged by trees below.

At the last second she darted left and curved her wings around her body. She dove like an arrow toward a grove of trees just east of her. Faster she fell, but she could still hear the hawk's screech. She beat her wings furiously until she reached the top branches. Then, in a move that had been bred into her species since they were tiny dinosaurs, she pointed with one wing skyward and the other at the earth. Through the branches she skimmed, alternating wings, flapping them with all her might as the adrenaline powered her instinctive response to danger. Just when her burning lungs were about to burst, she heard the distant call. The hawk was angry and frustrated. Being an open field hunter, it had broken off the chase and was now being chased itself by three angry redwing blackbirds.

She slowed, flared her wings and landed on a maple branch. As quickly as the chase had begun it was over. The adrenaline subsided and her hunger kicked in. It was time to find breakfast.

-20-
fiche

The Bismarck Police Department occupied the west half of the basement in the rundown library off Fifth Street at the edge of downtown Bismarck. It was a small clapboard room with wood floors that had been worn down by countless hobnail boots and more than a few sharp spurs worn by cowboys who thought coming to town was an excuse to drink cheap whiskey until their minds were numb and their mouths were big. Stale cigar smoke permeated the walls, sunk into the tattered wooden floors and the two holding cells smelled of dried vomit and pine tar soap.

The department had two doors, one in front that led to the street and the other one exactly opposite it that opened up into the county's dilapidated cottonwood log jail, a holdover from the late 19th Century.

Capt. Tom Thorson stormed in throwing his heavy woolen coat at a wall peg just inside the door. It caught and hung by the collar like it did every time he tossed it. In three steps he was behind his desk and sitting in his chair.

"Well?" he said to his secretary, Betty, as he blew on his hands to warm them.

"'Morning, Chief." She rose from her small desk, walked over to him and handed him a small piece of paper.

"Louise from Governor Shafer's Office called. Sounds important. She wants you to call her back right away."

Thorson picked up the black candlestick phone on his

desk and clicked the earpiece holder twice.

"Thelma," he said into the mouthpiece, "can ya please connect me to the state's operator."

Thorson leaned back in his chair and listened impatiently.

"I know they are all at the Grand Pacific Hotel, Thelma," he said sarcastically. "I sure did hear that the capitol burned down."

After what seemed like an hour, a voice at the other end answered.

"Good Morning, Rose, this is Tom Thorson. Put me through to Louise Bertram with the governor's office."

Thorson leaned forward and put his elbows on the desk.

"Lou! It's Tom. You called?"

Thorson listened for a few seconds. "How can they say that, Louise. Rags just don't start on fire." He stood up and listened intently for a few more seconds. "Aw, come on, Lou. The janitors used that ground-floor closet every day. Those rags ..."

He listened. The front door burst open and Elmer Black stormed in. Thorson motioned to him to be quiet.

"Okay, Lou. I know you're just the messenger. Thanks."

Thorson hung the earpiece back in the clicker and slammed the phone on his desk.

"So now you know, too," Black said.

"How'd you know?"

"Attorney general himself called. Told me their investigation found the cause to be something called 'spontaneous combustion' and to stop nosing around up there. It's official."

"The only thing official is how arrogant and stupid they are in state government."

"Tom, we only suspect arson. Can't prove it. And they've

started knocking down the remaining walls."

"Then we'd best get back up to the capitol and nose around some more. That fire was set and you know it, Black."

"I agree with you, Chief," Jake Tilden said from his perch in the far corner of the office.

Tilden, a small muscular man in his mid-thirties, wore Indian leggings over his knee-length riding boots, the latest style denim pants, and a crisp white linen shirt, which he had meticulously ironed himself. He had been a Burleigh County deputy sheriff until he was fired last year for beating Archibald Nelson, the town drunk, nearly to death. He had taken a swing at Tilden as he was being escorted from Miller's General Store and had paid dearly for it.

The beating wouldn't have mattered so much to Thorson if the drunk hadn't been the mayor's older brother. He was fairly harmless and roamed the streets of Bismarck winter and summer wearing the same long woolen coat. Although Nelson muttered to himself constantly, he never approached anyone, and was observed ignoring the taunting punk kids who relished in poking the man with sticks.

The mayor's brother ate what he could scrounge or what some church woman thrust into his hands, but occasionally he walked into a grocery store and helped himself to an apple, a transgression the store owner would ignore because the thief was the mayor's brother.

Early in the day he stumbled into Miller's General, Nelson had found and consumed nearly a full jar of moonshine partially hidden beneath a porch by the courthouse. Some kid had either dropped it or thrown it there to evade capture with the contraband, Nelson reasoned. "Never you mind, Archie, says I, their loz is your gain," he had mumbled. Then he had unscrewed the lid, smelled the acrid odor, and, in broad daylight, chugged the clear liquid, pausing only once to breathe and let out a whoop.

Fifteen minutes later, Nelson was reeling drunk, and stumbling around looking in every garbage can on his zig-zaggy hunt for a morsel to quiet the rumble in his belly. In a fit of alcoholic logic, he convinced himself that he deserved a meal of soda crackers and hard candy. He headed to the only place close where he could find open containers of his desired banquet – Miller's General Store.

When Ben Miller saw him stumble in, he immediately called the sheriff's office instead of the police. The police were afraid to do much because he was the mayor's brother. The county sheriff didn't have that problem.

Jake Tilden had been alone in the office when Miller called. He scribbled a note to the secretary, strapped on his holster for effect, pulled on his goat-skin gloves for protection from the beating he hoped to give, and headed smartly out the door. Grinning at what he was about to do, Tilden almost ran to Miller's General.

He arrived at the store out of breath and full of malice. Tilden hated the old drunk because the shithead couldn't control his drinking, ironically, any more than Tilden could control his temper.

As he stepped through the store's double doors, Miller waved his hand and pointed toward the middle of the store, with its neat rows of canned peaches, jars of pickled pigs feet, potted beef, and sacks of sugar and flour.

Tilden stomped toward the barrel of crackers and arrived just in time to see the mayor's brother stuffing crackers into his mouth with his left hand and his coat pocket with his right hand. Tilden had grabbed him by the back collar, which was so filthy that dried mud flaked off into the cracker barrel.

This fouling of the open food container, coupled with the swing the drunk took at him as he spun around, so angered Tilden that he almost strangled the man right in the store. But he waited.

He had dragged Nelson out of the store, down the steps, and around the side in the narrow space between Miller's General and the Patterson Hotel. There he had pummeled and kicked the man until his face looked like road kill. Just when he was about to plant a final blow to the man's temple with his boot heal, the cop on the beat had grabbed Tilden's own collar, pulled him away, and smacked him on the back of the head with his sap.

The blow from the leather-encased lead teardrop had knocked Tilden out cold. He had awakened in a jail cell with his head bandaged and his right wrist chained to the cot's metal frame. That's the position he was in when Thorson had walked in.

"We just can't have you beatin' our citizens," Thorson had said, "no matter who they are. I'm afraid I got to ask the sheriff to take away your badge."

A week or so later – Tilden couldn't ever remember how long he was in jail – a judge had let him off because they couldn't sober up Archie Nelson enough to testify; and the cop had told the court that he hadn't actually witnessed the beating, only stopped a kick to the drunk's head.

Tilden had then gone to work for the Morton County sheriff in Mandan, across the Missouri River, which was famous for being just north of Fort Abraham Lincoln, the location of George A. Custer's last home. The sheriff wouldn't hire him as a deputy, but as a special agent who hunted down and captured Indians who dared wander off the Standing Rock Indian Reservation looking for food or work; or, as Tilden was convinced, to rape young white girls. Of course they never did, but that was the excuse he used with regularity when he beat one into submission before dropping him off at the Morton County Jail. The Indian women he caught weren't so lucky.

Not only was Tilden vicious with them, he was sadistic. When he finished "just having a little fun wichya, little prairie piggy," he would drive them down to the edge of Fort Yates on the reservation and throw them out of his truck. But before he shoved them out, he would always grab their jaws in his gloved hand, look into their bruised, swollen eyes, and hiss, "I knows where you live, squaw, and if you tell anyone what I done, I'll come back and make you watch me kill your whole fucking family before I gut you like a deer, ya hear?"

What Tilden always failed to notice as he left the reservation was the same old Indian standing close to the side of a large boulder 50 feet from the road who watched him drive away.

The work gave Tilden a good physical workout and paid him just enough so he could afford to stay at a boarding house in Mandan and buy white shirts out of the Sears Roebuck catalogue.

Inevitably, though, Tilden would track a native across the Missouri River into Burleigh County. Tracking came easy to him. He had been a Pinkerton Detective Agency agent after the turn of the century. He rose fast in the ranks because he usually got his quarry. Pinkerton's didn't care about the quarry's condition when Tilden turned them in. Didn't care, that is, until the owners wanted to curry favor with the U.S. Secret Service by bringing to trial a gang that was counterfeiting 20-dollar bills and using them to pay for Canadian liquor they smuggled into the country. Tilden tracked them to a warehouse in northern Wisconsin and used several sticks of dynamite to blow the place to smithereens along with all the gang members except a young woman who had gone out back to pee in the woods near the warehouse. She died later.

Following the explosion, Tilden circled the building looking for tracks of anyone who might have escaped the blast. That's when he saw her, picking herself up on the opposite side of a large pine tree that had obviously shielded her from flying glass and bricks.

The building had turned into an inferno, so Tilden didn't want to have his fun with her there. He wrenched her off the ground, slapped shackles on her wrists, and dragged her kicking and screaming into the woods. She fought him, scratching at his face and trying to bite his ears and nose. Finally, after a vicious beating, she submitted.

Two days later, they boarded the train for Washington, D.C. Somewhere east of Illinois, she fell from the train. The circumstances were sketchy. Tilden said she tried to escape when he was sleeping. The train conductor said that would have been difficult seeing as how her hands and feet were shackled.

They found her body the next day, a hundred yards from the tracks. Her face was battered, her hair was matted with blood, and deep scratches covered her arms and hands. The sheriff on the scene said the fall from the train onto the jagged rocks killed her. How she was able to get that far from the tracks no one knew, but they all were curious about boot prints next to the body until Tilden explained in great detail how he had tracked her there before returning to the train stop and calling the sheriff's office to report he had found her body.

Plausible enough, the sheriff thought. Pinkerton's knew better. Tilden's reputation as a skilled tracker ranked second only to his skill as a liar. It was a known fact that he would just as soon lie as tell the truth, even when the truth suited him better. His proclivities for mistreating women were well known, but ignored.

This time, though, Tilden cost Pinkerton's a huge Federal government contract. The Secretary of the Treasury and the Attorney General wouldn't even meet with the Pinkerton's delegation to hear its explanation of why the Federal government wouldn't have a counterfeiting gang member to try as an example to others who might consider taking on the combined law enforcement might of the United States.

Pinkerton's sent Tilden a terse telegram ending his employment.

```
To: J. Tilden Lincoln Hotel
Your services are terminated. Stop.
Pinkerton's
```

When he read it, he drove a gloved fist through the hotel room wall and headed out in search of a speakeasy and a younger teenage girl.

Three weeks later, when his money was running out and word got around to the local whores to stay away from him, Tilden bought a one-way ticket on a west-bound train as far as his money would take him. The ticket agent laughed when he sold Tilden a ticket to Bismarck, North Dakota, a place, he said, had barely evolved from its days as a cow town.

When he got off the train in Bismarck on July 21, 1925,

Tilden walked the two blocks north to the Burleigh County Courthouse, walked into the sheriff's office, and told them he was a recently retired, highly respected Pinkerton agent who had come west to combat lawlessness and the evils of illegal alcohol.

-21-

fiche a haon

Bismarck, North Dakota
December 31, 1930

Police Chief Tom Thorson slid his feet off the desk in the front office of the Bismarck Police Department. The desk was cluttered with files waiting for someone's attention. Fire Chief Elmer Black sat on a chair in a corner opposite Thorson. Thorson slowly shook his head. "That's serious, Elmer. Why would somebody deliberately burn down the Capitol?"

"If I knew that, Tom, you and I'd already be talking to likely culprits, now wouldn't we?"

"You know them boys in the attorney general's office ain't gonna believe it. Tell me again why you think it was arson," Thorson said.

Black's neck was getting redder. He hated being challenged and was fed up with the cop's disbelief, "First off, Thomas, where was the goddamn night watchman? He should have been able to put out any fire before it got hold of the whole damn building, right?"

"Now, EB, I'm just playin' whatcha call your 'devil's advocate' here. What if he had just finished his rounds and gone to the basement to sit a spell and roll a smoke? Or, what if he was at the northwest corner of the top floor?"

"Wouldn't matter. Them fellas make rounds every half

hour. That fire took at least forty-five minutes to get to where Eli called it in."

"What about Eli? Could he have started it?"

"Black, he's the high school's English teacher. Besides, he'd had so much eggnog in him he woulda caught fire himself."

"Where was the night watchman?"

"Let's find out," Black said.

~22~

FICHE A DÓ

The road was icy and O'Connor's mood was as grey as the winter sky above them. They had been driving for hours in the cold with scant heat coming into the cab from the pickup's meager heater. They approached one more small hill on the far side of a small lake, and O'Connor shifted the truck into second gear. The motor groaned as the truck lumbered up the rise. At the crest, O'Connor saw a small town nestled in the valley below. Snow began to fall, lightly at first, and then the flakes got as big as white rose petals.

"Pretty," Brigid said.

"Guess so," replied O'Connor. In all his twenty-nine years he had never been able to understand why some people liked the stuff. To him snow usually meant misery. Miserable marching. Miserable sleeping. Miserable meals.

He looked over at her. She had pulled her hair back and tied it together so it stayed out of her face. Even in the dim light he could appreciate her clean beauty and the shape of her lips which were full but not overly so. He imagined kissing them …

"Look out!"

His distracted driving and newly fallen snow had the truck in a slide toward the ditch. He turned the steering wheel hard and almost rolled it over.

"Are you trying to kills us," she shrieked.

O'Connor recovered his composure and stared straight

ahead. "Better find a place to bed down," he said.

Brigid looked at him, weary and frightened. "If this damn truck and its driver can make it," she sighed sarcastically.

O'Connor just stared ahead trying to see the road through the snow, too angry to stop as they drove through the town they'd spotted while cresting the hill.

An hour later, Brigid waited at the front door of a hotel in Jamestown, 100 miles east of Bismarck. She leaned over and looked into the large window next to the door. The little lobby was dimly lit and the place looked deserted. O'Connor bumped into her when he walked to the door.

"Go in, Lass. Go in!"

O'Connor pushed her through the door and the smell of rose water and dust hit them at once. He scanned the lobby, noticed the yellowed floral wall coverings and the worn upholstery on chairs in the corner. Out of habit he planned three escape routes: he was on the threshold of one, another through a side window, the third out the back hall.

He and Brigid walked up to the unattended front desk. Hand written on a faded and frayed sign on the wall was "Ring Bell fer maneger." Brigid impatiently pounded her hand on the rusting bell sitting on the scarred wood counter and O'Connor twirled the registration book, picked up the pencil that was attached to its spine with bailing twine, and began to fill it out.

A sleepy elderly man shuffled out of the door behind the desk. "Help ya?"

"Me'n the lady here are cold and tired."

The old man twirled the book back and looked down.

"Only got one room left. Big one with three beds. Somebody else comes, you'll hafta share. You lovebirds won't mind, now will you, Mr. and Mrs. O'Flare-ah-tye?"

His stale liquor-tobacco-coffee breath competed with the smell of dust on his clothes and cheap aftershave to nauseate Brigid.

O'Connor corrected him. "It's O'Flahrtee."

The old man snorted his disgust and reached for the only key on the board behind him.

"Top floor, to your right, last door on the left. Bathroom's at the head of the steps. Check out at ten, or it's a dollar an hour. Watch out for the banister. It ain't safe."

O'Connor and Brigid headed up the creaky stairs, she lugging the leather duffle bag, he with no luggage. They walked down the narrow hall to their room, boots clunking on the well-worn wood slat floors. A small brass plate crudely tacked on the fourth door's peeling paint identified their room.

O'Connor fumbled with the key in his right hand, turned the doorknob, reached inside, and turned the round light switch on the wall. Proximity to a woman other than a Chicago waitress rattled him.

Inside the large square room a lone light bulb dangled on a twisted cord from the ceiling. A knotted rope lay curled by the room's only window. There were three beds in three corners. A rocking chair and small table occupied the corner closest to the window.

"The King's Palace!" Brigid chortled, as she walked in.

O'Connor closed the door and surveyed the room, again planning their escape. "If the King was here, I'd kill 'im and 'is whole murderin' family."

"That's tough talk for a penniless Irishman stuck in the middle of America," she said.

O'Connor picked the bed in the outside corner nearest the rope. He looked out the window and then down at the rope. Brigid went to the bed in the opposite corner nearest the door. She threw her bag on the floor and tested the mattress with one hand. The bed squeaked, but satisfied she hopped on the bed, laced her fingers behind her head and watched O'Connor.

He kicked at the rope on the floor. "Dont'cha feel safer, now, knowing we've got a fire escape?"

"I doubt we'd have enough time to open the window and throw out the rope. This old tinderbox'd go up in minutes with the right wind," she observed.

O'Connor glanced at her and turned to gaze out the window. He removed his hat, put his face close to the window and cupped his hands around his eyes. All he could see was snow blowing sideways. "We got us a raging snow storm," he said to the window. "Hope you got enough money to hold this room for a few days."

In the dim light reflected on the window, O'Connor saw Brigid slip a gun under her pillow.

"I'm not spending my time in this dump," she said. She rose from the bed and walked to the window. She imitated O'Connor's technique of cupping her hands around her eyes to look out the window. "Where'd the town go?"

"It's still out there, just covered with snow."

"How are you going to get us out of here?"

"How am I going to get us out of her? Lass, you're wearing pants. Expensive ones, too, by the looks of it. I'm sure you'll find a way."

Brigid turned from the window and jumped on the bed again causing it to squeak and the bedsprings to hit the floor. O'Connor watched her reflection in the window. He wondered when she would make her move. When he slept? That was the most logical, he thought. Put a pillow over the gun to deaden the sound. But his instincts honed in war would let him sense the closeness of her in the dead of night.

When she had laid her head on the pillow again, he turned from the window, removed his coat, and hung it and his hat on a square iron nail that had been pounded into the rough clapboard wall. He eased onto the bed, removed his boots to reveal worn grey socks with holes in the toes. His large knife hung in plain sight from his belt. Brigid stared at the knife.

"Don't worry, Lassy. If I wanted to kill you, I'd a done it at your car when I figured out it was you who poked a hole in the gas tank."

"What do you mean? I never…"

O'Connor rose from the bed and walked to the door. He closed it and turned the lock.

"Nothing on a road makes a nice round hole. Besides, your front tire more'n likely would have been punctured first. So, if I was going to hurt you, I'd have done it out in the middle of nowhere, not in a hotel in a town with coppers."

Brigid slowly reached under her pillow.

"Do not do that. You will not need your gun for protection."

Brigid moved her hands back behind her head. She tried to look nonchalant, but was amazed and frightened that O'Connor knew about the pistol.

"I saw you slip that little cannon under your pillow," he revealed. "Besides, I'd have this knife through that pretty little neck of yours before you could take aim."

At that, Brigid shoved her hand under the pillow and pulled the derringer out. In a flash, O'Connor was across the room. He grabbed her arm and with his left hand twisted the small pistol out of her hand. Then he slapped her. Hard.

Dazed, she rubbed the left side of her face where he had struck her. Her ear rang and blood started to trickle from her mouth. She could barely hear what he was saying.

"Must be a train come through here soon. You take the first one out," O'Connor ordered. Then he opened the derringer and popped out the cartridges. He put the derringer in his pants pocket. He looked around the room and walked to the window keeping one eye on her. He opened the window and was going to throw the bullets into the snow below but thought better of it. He didn't want any children to find them once the snow melted. Then he noticed a gap in the window sill. As snow blew into the room, O'Connor dropped the small bullets down inside the wall and quickly closed the window. He turned to her.

"Got any more bullets?"

"No."

He grabbed the bag on her bed and opened it. She sprang up and reached for the bag. He shoved her back down. Then he put his hand up with his palm toward her as if commanding a dog. "Sit!"

She obeyed, and lightly rubbed her cheek. The speed and force of the slap had caught her off guard. Unlike in a boxing ring, where she would have been prepared to ward off blows, her training had not prepared her for the reality of a lightning-fast slap when she least expected it. She would fix that when she got home.

O'Connor rummaged through her bag. After pushing undergarments out of the way, he pulled out a large wad of money, looked at it and stuffed it back in the bag. Then his fingers found what he knew was there. He pulled out the small box of ammunition.

"Your Da teach you to lie, darlin'?"

O'Connor strode to his bed and put the box of shells into his coat pocket. He wearily laid down on the bed and stared at Brigid. "I told you I wouldn't kill you, darlin'. Hungry?"

His familiarity was grating on her. "Yes," she said through clenched teeth.

O'Connor reached into his coat pocket and pulled out a small package wrapped in oily brown paper. Untying the string, he opened it and picked out a piece of withered dried meat. He took a bite and then picked up another piece and threw it across the room. It hit the wall and fell on Brigid's bed.

"Is this all we have to eat?" she complained.

"No fancy Dans to bring a four-course meal to the room. You hungry, you eat. If you don't want it, I'll have it back."

Brigid slowly gnawed off a bite. Her jaw burned and popped as she chewed. O'Connor rose from the bed, walked to the light switch and looked over at Brigid.

"Stay put."

"Don't flatter yourself."

O'Connor smiled as he turned off the light. He took the five steps across the dark room to his bed. He propped up the pillow against the wall and pulled his buffalo coat over him. He drew the knife out of its sheath and laid it on his lap. Folding his arms across his chest, he closed his eyes and wondered who had sent her to kill him.

Seething in the darkness, her pride hurt more than her cheek, Brigid continued to slowly chew the meat as she tried to think of when, where, and how she would kill O'Connor. The "why" was to make Da proud of her for once.

-23-

fiche a trí

Bismarck
January 1, 1931

The three days following the fire that leveled North Dakota's capitol had been chaotic for politicians, bureaucrats, residents, but especially the Bismarck police.

Rumors ran rampant: Renegade Indians started the fire in retaliation for Sitting Bull's murder; the Ku Klux Klan burned it down to divert attention from their anti-papist campaign; a ball of lightning struck and ran through the building; German immigrants or Scandinavians or a band of Gypsies did it just to get even – for what no one could figure out or say. Some agricultural college kid home for the holidays even called the police claiming the fire could have been caused by something called 'spontaneous combustion'. Captain Thorson wondered what kind of hooch college kids were brewing in frat houses.

Worst of it all, the only cause that Thorson and the Fire Chief thought was plausible was that some idiot just might have lit a cigar and dropped the smoldering match into a wastebasket full of paper. The two of them swore they were determined to find the cause, or at least eliminate all the rumors.

Thorson and Black sat in their respective places. Ed Smith, one of the night watchmen at the capitol, sat nervously in a straight-backed chair facing the policeman.

"Now Ed, none of the other fellas were on duty."

"'Cept for Nagel," Black intoned from behind the watchman.

Smith turned his head and shoulders quickly to look at the fire chief. Then he turned back to Thorson.

"Right. Like I told ya. I asked Nagel to switch with me so I could be with my Ma. Then I ..."

"Must be hard on her, what with your father dyin' right before Thanksgiving," Thorson said. "I'm real sorry."

"Nagel says Hank Thomas called him, told him he was gonna work that night."

Smith turned around to Black.

"He ... he called me, too!"

"Look at me, Ed," Thorson said. "We've talked to every one of the watchmen. We haven't talked to a Hank Thomas, Ed."

Smith's voice broke and sweat beaded his forehead. "I'd never heard of him either. Nagel said he was a new hand and they wanted him to practice the routine during the holidays when it would be real quiet."

"So you take orders from a greenhorn?"

"My Ma needed me! What's going on here?"

"Some sons-a-bitch bur ..." Black's frustration came through.

Thorson glared at him over the watchman's shoulder and gave him a quick tick of his head that said be quiet. Then he looked Smith in the eyes and talked to him in a calming voice. "Nothing, Ed. Ain't nothin' going on. Me and Chief Black are just trying to find out what happened, that's all. You go home to your Ma, now. Tell her I said I'm real sorry for her loss."

Smith got up and his left calf caught under the seat. The chair fell over and hit the floor with a loud bang, which made him jump like a scared jackrabbit. Head hung to the side, he glanced at Black and then hurried out of the office.

Thorson glared at Black and snarled, "What were you trying to do, Chief? You put it out that somebody burned that building on purpose, the whole town will know before Amos and Andy comes on the radio. Pretty soon, the whole damn state knows."

"Maybe somebody saw something, detective."

"And maybe whoever mighta done it slips outta town before we can find out they're the one," Thorson counter punched and smiled.

"Now what about this Hank Thomas?" Black asked, sensing that his sarcasm had been too cutting.

"There ain't no Hank Thomas, Elmer. I talked to one of the gals in the governor's office I know. She checked around for me. Nobody ever heard of Hank Thomas. He don't exist. You done real good."

"Well, then, we'd best take a good look around the capitol grounds. See what we can see," smiled Black, "and hope lots of folks watch our effort."

-24-

fiche a ceathair

"Shit, Tilden's here," Thorson said as he and Black drove onto the capitol grounds. The smoldering remains of the capital building stared down at them from the top of the slope. They pulled off at the entrance to the grounds, parked the car next to Jake Tilden's truck, and walked over to the earth lodge. When they walked in, they saw Tilden on all fours sniffing the dirt floor.

"Somebody swept a pine bough over the ground here," Tilden said not looking up.

"No way you can smell pine on that dirt floor," Black said.

"Don't need to," Tilden replied looking up. "There's pine needles here and there."

"So?"

"So, chief, somebody tried to cover their tracks. Pretty damn good job, too. But I'm trained to look for the slightest clue. Pinkerton's dun that for me, at least," Tilden said.

"Coulda been kids," Thorson said.

"Coulda been," Tilden said, "but why? Ain't no kids gonna do nothin' here. Too cold."

"Unless they was drinkin' and messin' around," Black said. "My kid's always lookin' for a place to get his gal friends drunk."

"When he has a snoot full of moonshine," Tilden asked, "is he smart enough to sweep over their tracks right out the door?"

"'Suppose not."

The three men walked out of the lodge and into the blazing winter sun made even brighter shining through a cloudless azure sky and reflecting off the snow-covered ground.

"So you're sayin' someone covered up the fact that they been here," said Thorson.

"Right, and then they took off toward the capitol."

"Didn't no one see them," Black asked.

"Don't know," said Tilden, "'cause that ain't my job to find out. I just think that someone hid here 'til darkest part of the night, then walked hisself to the capitol and burned it down."

While the police chief and fire chief drove over to the west edge of the grounds and went door to door asking people what, if anything, they saw the night of the fire, Tilden followed a path from the earth lodge to the smoldering building. He stopped at a bush beside the impromptu path and sniffed around the bottom branches before heading up to the north side of the building.

He searched there until he found footprints heading away from the site. He was standing at that spot when Black and Thorson walked to his position.

"Well," Tilden asked.

"No one heard or saw nothin'," Thorson said, "just like I figured."

"'Cept I had one fella say he saw a wolf or a big dog or a bear running toward the capitol after it peed at a bush," Black said, "but his wife yelled from the kitchen that he'd been drinking eggnog all night, so he should just shut up and close the damn door. Thought I was going to have a home disturbance for you to break up, Thorson."

"He probably did see something that looked like a big

animal," Tilden said. "I traced the path from the lodge to the building here and saw scraping alongside footprints, probably by a long fur coat. I even sniffed at that bush 'cause the tracks stopped there before heading on. There weren't no smell of animal pee there, and the snow around it weren't yellow, neither," Tilden said.

"So that fella was suffering alcohol-induced visions," Thorson said. He and Black laughed.

"Someone burned this place down," Tilden said emphatically.

"We ain't got no proof, Tilden," Black said.

They were quiet for a few minutes. Thorson scanned the scene, looked down the slope to the earth lodge, over to the houses lining Fourth Street and then back to Black and Tilden.

"Chief," he addressed Black, avoiding Tilden's eyes, "you got any reason we shouldn't call this an accident and get on with our lives?"

"Nope," replied Black.

"Bullshit," said Tilden. I'm going to catch me an arsonist, and when I do, I 'spect the governor is going to give me a big fuckin' reward."

"You do whatever you think you gotta do," Thorson warned him, "within the law. Got it?"

"Fuck you and the law and your bullshit investigation," Tilden said and stomped back down the slope to his truck.

Black and Thorson stayed behind until they were sure Tilden wasn't going to look back at them, and couldn't see them even if he did. Thorson handed Black an oiled brown envelope. "I told Stratford we wouldn't find any evidence or witnesses. He kept his word. Here's your cut."

Black stuffed the envelope inside his coat. "Happy New Year, chief," he said to Thorson.

-25-

fIChe λ cúIG

The storm swept down from Canada during the night. Tilden woke up in his small boarding house room, shivering from the severe January cold snap. He glanced outside through the threadbare curtain covering his only window.

Seeing the blizzard, he swore and pulled up the covers that he had kicked off during the night and stuffed his head under the pillow.

His grip was by the door, ready for the train ride east. After he had walked away from those two assholes Black and Thorson, Tilden had driven around to the gravel road north of the capitol where he found footprints coming from the capitol to tire tracks that only headed east. Following the tracks as far as his eyes could see he made up his mind that he was right about arson. He, Jake Tilden, highly experienced Pinkerton agent, was just the skilled tracker who was going to find the culprit.

He would show those two assholes, even if it meant weeks of tracking and maybe even bringing home a head in a basket. But if he brought just a head, how could he prove it had belonged to the arsonist? I know, he thought as he got back in his truck and started driving to Mandan, I'll torture the bastard until he signs a confession before I kill him and cut off his head for proof.

After packing his grip with all his clothes, including four neatly folded starched white dress shirts, he sat at the small table in his room and did some figuring. He knew the train was the best way for someone who had committed a serious crime to escape and since there were few major stops going east, Tilden figured he would take the train, too; and ask around at each stop if anyone had seen a person wearing a long animal-skin coat.

This goddamn storm would delay his departure for a few days, but by god, I'll prove I'm right. Bastards!

Two days later, Tilden boarded the eastbound train in Mandan. His first long stop would be in a place these hicks called Jamestown. Then Valley City. Then Fargo. It was going to be a long trip and take him a long time, but he was going to prove he was right about arson. Then Pinkerton would have to hire him back. They might even beg for his forgiveness.

-26-

fιϽϧε Ͻ sé

Ft. Yates, North Dakota
January 4, 1931

Today is the day, the old Lakota decided. He would avenge his granddaughter, restore her dignity, and stop the shit eating dog of a white man from ever again hurting any young girl in his tribe. It was time to resurrect the warrior.

A Lakota Sioux, he had been born in a teepee sometime around 1860, he thought. His early life consisted of learning how to ride a pony, hunting rabbits and prairie chickens, playing rough and tumble games, and making his own bow and arrows and then practicing shooting them until his fingers bled. When he turned 14, he had to learn to shoot while riding his pony so he might one day kill a running Tatanka or an invading Cree warrior. In doing so, he was idolized by his younger siblings, especially Little Bear, his little brother.

At the age of 16, his father and uncle let him come with them to a large gathering of Lakota, Northern Cheyenne, and Arapaho tribes in Montana Territory.

The atmosphere there was electric. He was so excited that he danced around constantly, yelling battle cries with the warriors, until he couldn't resist sleep so he reluctantly crawled into his father's teepee and collapsed. When he awoke the next morning in the empty teepee, he scrambled outside and saw that his father and uncles and their horses were painted for battle.

"What's happening," the boy asked his father.

"We're going to win a big victory over the white eyes today," he replied.

The boy looked around. He stood in the midst of hundreds of mounted warriors, all whose faces were painted in black stripes and dressed in their finest war costumes.

"Where's my pony," the boy yelled to no one.

"You stay here," his father said as he leaned down from his horse and held the boy's chin in his rough hand. "Watch from that ridge," he pointed up to a small rock outcropping. "You'll be safe there."

"I don't want to be safe," the boy yelled to his father as he and his uncles rode to join the others who were preparing for battle.

Unable to find his horse, the boy did as he was told. He watched from the ridge as the white man's cavalry charged, circled their horses, and died in the hot Montana sun.

When the dust finally settled on the battlefield, the boy walked down the hill to the encampment and waited for his father and uncles to regale him with tales of the battle. They never came. He waited alone until dusk the next day. Finally, a sweat and dust-covered warrior from his village with bloody scalps hanging from his spear approached leading the boy's pony.

"You need to come," he said.

"Come where," the boy asked.

"North, away from this place. Your father is with his ancestors."

So the boy and a small troop of Cheyenne and Lakota trekked north some 15 miles behind Sitting Bull, who was fleeing to Canada.

When his band got a safe distance into Canada, the boy lived a rough life for three years with the small group of Indians, hunting small game and catching fish when he could.

One day as he was trying to spear fish in a stream over a hill from their camp, he heard women scream and voices were yelling at his people, "R-C-M-P! Drop your weapons! We won't hurt you!"

The boy crawled up the embankment over the stream and watched as the small group of warriors, women, and children were rounded up by men in red coats and big hats and marched away from the camp, leaving empty teepees and smoldering fires.

When he was sure they were gone and that he could not be seen, he snuck into the camp, gathered as much dried elk meat and clothing as he could carry, and headed south, home.

The year was 1879, and for 72 days the boy walked, always with the sun on his left in the morning and on his right in the afternoons after he ate his midday meal and slept a short while.

Finally, thin and with sore feet poking through holes in his moccasins, he reached the Ft. Peck Reservation where he knew he would be welcomed by the Yanktonai Sioux. He was more than welcomed by a comely young woman, who he met one night at a dance competition, and who didn't seem to mind that he, Black Wolf, was a Lakota, especially when he repeated his stories about witnessing the battle that the whites now called the Custer Massacre and his years living off the land in Canada.

She was so impressed by his bravery that she happily

agreed to marry him after he finally proposed the following fall. Two years after their wedding, the white man's government forced the Yanktonai and anyone connected to them to join others of their tribe at Ft. Yates in Dakota Territory, which ironically was close to where Custer and his army had lived.

After the whites took away everyone's firearms, Black Wolf became an expert marksman with a bow, and a craftsman of fine hunting knives in the town where no one wanted to live – and beyond. He supported his growing family by hunting for fresh meat to replace the hated meat in jars the tribe got from the Indian Agent. People from all over came to buy his knives, which came to command high prices. One day, a smelly old mountain man from Montana, he said, rode into town on a wooly horse trailing a scrawny pack mule that was loaded with beaver pelts, the last in Montana, he said. He asked specifically to see the Black Wolf who made hunting knives, and when he rode up to Black Wolf's government-supplied log house, he dismounted and in a tired voice, asked Black Wolf if they could talk privately. Inside, the mountain man said he had lost his last friend, his woman had died of dysentery, couldn't trap any more beaver 'cause there weren't none, and besides, he was just plain wore out, so could Black Wolf trade him four hunting knives for a special item.

"Depends on the item," Black Wolf had said. So the mountain man went to his pack mule and led it up to the door and made it stand sideways so it blocked any view of the door. He then pulled a Sharps rifle from a scabbard underneath the beaver pelts.

"Does it shoot straight," Black Wolf asked the mountain man.

"Depends on the shooter," he replied.

"Two knives," said Black Wolf.

"Five and I'll throw in two boxes of shells."

"You bargain too well. What would I do without shells?"

"Hang it over your mantle and wish you had them."

And so, Black Wolf became the proud owner of a contraband Sharps rifle.

Twenty years later, here he was, out of sight of his wife of 31 summers, in their small bedroom, dressed in his finest woolen pants, red suspenders and checkered lumberjack shirt. His face was chiseled by relentless prairie winds, bright summer sun, and deep sadness. Except for long gray hair he tied in a ponytail so he could shove it under his hat, he looked like every other Indian who had grown up dressing to fit in the White Man's world. Picking his clothing was not the reason he didn't want the woman to see what he was up to, though.

Inside his pants just behind the right front pocket he had hidden his large trade knife. He had honed it razor sharp the previous day in his shack out back, where his woman knew she was unwelcome. The woman always knew he was up to something in that drafty old shack. He didn't like hiding things from her, but being able to chew and smoke tobacco without her angry looks just made life easier. He knew she knew what he did there, but it was her unspoken acceptance that made him love her more after all these years.

In his private realm, he only sharpened his axe so wood cutting was easier. Yesterday, though, he had sharpened his trade knife to make cutting out the skinny little white man's heart easier. He had other knives – a curved hunting knife he used for skinning animals and a small pocketknife he used for odd jobs, but he displayed the trade knife on the shack's wall to remind him of better, freer days when his only interaction with whites was when they could gain something from each other. Soon he would reclaim some self respect and the Evil One would gain freedom from this world for what he had been doing to the young girls in Ft. Yates and who knows where else.

As he worked the trade knife's blade sharper and sharper, he thought about his brother who had fled the reservation two years ago after an altercation with a BIA Policeman. Seven months later his brother sent him a short letter telling him that he was in Chicago working as a janitor in a Catholic mission and living in the basement. Could he please send money? That was all the old Lakota knew. He and the woman didn't have enough money to share, but they did own something of value that might help.

The previous winter, the old Lakota rode his horse into the hills west of Ft. Lincoln, which was northeast of Ft. Yates, to see if he could find the lone Tatanka he had seen roaming about in the fall. He was lucky enough to pick up the buffalo's trail and after tracking his prey several miles, he easily spotted the dark shape in the glaring snow standing next to a bare burr oak at the crest of a small hill.

He left his horse in a ravine, crept to the top of a small rise, and fired one shot from his old Sharps. He watched the old animal waver then fall to its knees. He got up, brushed the snow off his breeches and coat, peered one more time at the dark shape at the foot of the tree, turned and walked back to his horse, put the Sharp's in its sheath, and rode to claim his kill. On the one hand, he was sad because the old Tatanka was alone and he didn't enjoy killing as much as he did the hunt. However, the hide would make a warm coat and he and his tribe would have real meat for part of the winter instead of the stringy potted beef the government supplied.

When he received the letter from his brother asking for money, the old Lakota asked his wife if he could send his brother the coat they had made from the buffalo hide. She agreed because, like her husband, she believed that giving today meant getting tomorrow. He built a special wooden crate to hold the coat and used his neighbor's horse team and wagon to cart it to the train depot in Mandan where he gladly paid two dollars to ship it to his brother at the St. Nicholas Catholic Mission in Chicago.

Finished with the memory of the memory, he stuffed his bankroll into his knee-length winter moccasins he had made from two beaver pelts, unlocked the bedroom door and walked into the living area. His wife noticed his clothing. She knew not to ask, but couldn't help herself.

"Why are you dressed like that," she asked.

"Goin' into Mandan to buy you a present."

"You're lying."

"Then don't be so nosey, old woman."

"It's starting to snow. You better not go."

"The horse knows the way if the snow comes too hard."

"Be careful."

He put on his warmest winter coat, tucked his hair up under his fur hat, picked up a large hat box and small satchel, walked out to the horse corral, threw on the saddle and Sharps rifle, cursed the weather, and headed north.

The snowstorm grew into a full-blown blizzard, but his horse plodded along and the man simply pulled his head down to his shoulders like a frightened turtle. By the time horse and rider got close to Mandan, they looked like a moving snow statue. The Lakota stopped at a small farmhouse, owned by a boyhood friend, at the edge of town, dismounted and pulled his horse into the barn. They would hold up there until the storm blew over. What he thought would be one night turned into three days.

He was able to trudge through the snow banks to the farmhouse where his only white friend lived, and was able to pass the time with the couple talking about playing cowboys and Indians together as children, wrestling on the grass, and attending country dances in a neighbor's barn.

Three days after he pulled his horse into the barn, the trip from the farm into downtown Mandan took him most of one day. Snow was piled everywhere in the town, which made navigating the gravel streets difficult. He arrived at the boarding house where he knew the Evil One lived. Last fall he had gone to town late one afternoon to buy his granddaughter a new dress to lift her spirits and happened to see the skinny white man enter the front door of the place. A few seconds later, Black Wolf noticed a second-story window suddenly glow later. Today would be the Evil one's last day on earth.

The old Lakota tied his horse to a railing across the street from the boarding house and went into the general store, one of the few places he was allowed to go in this town where people still talked about the day Pehin hanska, Long Hair, their General Custer, headed to Montana and death.

"Whatcha need, Black Wolf," the elderly store owner asked through teeth clenched on the soggy end of a half-smoked cigar.

Thinking quickly because he only went into the store to thaw his fingers and toes, Black Wolf said, "Looking for a can of cherry preserves." He knew the store only received one shipment of the jam from Michigan in the spring.

"Sold the last can months ago. Won't get more for four months. I can put one aside for you if you like."

"That would be good. Thanks. Mind if I look around?"

"Nope, go ahead. But if I get another customer, I'd ask you to leave real quick-like."

Black Wolf rubbed his fingers together as he strode quietly through the aisles between shelves of pots and pans and saws and hammers and sacks of flour and sugar and big cans of something called peanut butter and dresses and shirts and candy canes and horse tack. His wanderings brought him back to the front door with warmed hands and thawed toes, so he tried to quietly slip out, but the small bell nailed over the door clanged. When he heard the tinkle, the store owner glanced up from his paperwork to see if he had a paying customer who would be uncomfortable shopping with an Indian in the store. Seeing Black Wolf leave, he shifted his cigar to the other side of his mouth and went back to figuring out what to order for the coming months.

The Lakota shivered from the frigid temperature as he trudged across the snow covered street, now gouged with tire tracks. Inside the boarding house, he quietly walked up the stairs and rounded the stair railing. When he approached the Evil One's room, he reached inside his pants at the back and grasped the handle of his trade knife. Just then a voice called out behind him.

"If you're looking for Tilden," the female voice said with a thick Norwegian accent, "he's gone. Skedaddled out on the eastbound train yesterday right after he got a visit from a tall, scary lookin' fella."

Black Wolf turned to look at her.

"Headed?"

"Well, like I just told you, someplace out East."

"Coming back?"

"I kinda doubt that since he took all his belongings and paid his bill. Oh, and you gotta leave my house. Now!"

Without a word, Black Wolf walked past the wiry woman glaring at him in the hall, went down the stairs and out the door. Today would not be the day. He had prepared to run away after killing the Evil One, but that also meant Black Wolf was prepared to track him down.

Out in the cold again, he looked over at his horse, which was now stomping its feet and shivering to stay warm. He knew the horse knew his way home, so when they got to the railroad depot, Black Wolf removed his belongings from the saddlebags, which held some jerky and rolled-up buckskins, a large hat box in which he had placed his ceremonial war bonnet that many white people thought all Indians wore all the time; and a buckskin case that he had rigged up with an old bow tip and a couple of broken arrow tops to disguise its real content – his Sharp's rifle and ammunition. He pushed his horse's neck and slapped her rear, telling her to go home.

He carried his strange belongings into the depot, put them next to a bench, and bought a ticket on the next day's east-bound train. Then he waited.

His plan after killing the Evil One was to ride north into Canada and join a Wild West Show where he could blend in with natives from other tribes. He might even get away with murder, but he knew eventually the authorities there would catch him and turn him over to the BIA. Its agents would probably kill him on the spot like they had Tatánka Íyotake, who the Whites had called Sitting Bull. Black Wolf believed in his heart that killing the Evil One would be worth the dying because it would lift the spirits of so many young women. All he had to do now was catch the skinny bastard.

It would be difficult, he knew, because the man had a day's head start. At each stop Black Wolf would ask if anyone had seen a skinny man with greasy slicked-back hair and wearing a starched white shirt get off the train.

Black Wolf sat upright on the wooden bench, closely watching his belongings. For 13 hours he didn't slouch or lay down. He just waited, back straight and stiff like a lodge pole. He stood only when he wanted a drink or to relieve himself. No one bothered him. Indians traveling by train was a common occurrence in this land.

When the train finally pulled in, it sat on the tracks for two hours taking on fuel and cargo. The crew got off and a new crew replaced them. When the train and crew were ready, the station manager called the passengers to board.

"Train to Fargo, St. Cloud and St. Paul now departing," he yelled into the waiting room, "All aboard!"

Black Wolf calmly waited as seven other passengers left the station waiting room and boarded. He knew they wanted to sit as far away from him as possible, and that suited him just fine. The white women reeked of strong rose water and the white men just plain reeked.

On the train, seeing that the passenger car was not crowded, he picked a seat next to the door, placed his hat box and saddle bags in the overhead space, and carefully set his buckskin case's butt end on the floor next to him.

When the train stopped in Valley City to pick up passengers and load freight, Black Wolf only picked up his rifle case and carried it off the train and into the depot.

"Why do you want him," the station manager asked him, skeptically. It was unusual for an Indian to be asking about a white man.

"He's my partner in our act in a wild west show," Black

Wolf explained. "I play Sitting Bull and he plays Buffalo Bill."

"How's come you ain't traveling together?"

"I got too drunk on moonshine after the last place and he got mad at me and left," an out and out lie because he never drank alcohol but knew this white man believed no Indian could hold his fire water, illegal or otherwise.

"Yep, he was here. Funny thing, though. He was asking about anyone wearing a long buffalo coat. Why would he do that?"

Black Wolf thought for a minute. It was getting easier to lie, and lying to white men was even enjoyable.

"The man in the buffalo coat is … um … the boss of Colonel Wood's Wild West Show. We're gonna meet him in Chicago."

"Never heard of that one."

"It's new."

"Your boss was traveling with a woman …"

"She plays Annie Oakley," he made up on the spot. This was great fun, he thought. And the lies sounded completely believable.

"Well, they left the day before your partner got here. They were real friendly with each other when they got on the train, too."

"She's his woman."

"Your train's leaving."

Black Wolf grabbed his buckskin case by the rifle barrel and started to walk out of the station.

"Is that really your bow and arrows?"

"What?"

"I meant, is that a real Indian bow and arrows?"

"I use it to shoot a brass ring out of Annie's hand while I'm riding my war pony at a full gallop. The arrow then hits a bull's eye behind her."

The awe-struck man looked at him. "Don't say."

A smiling Black Wolf turned and hurried across the platform and back to his seat. He settled in and watched the snow piles go slowly by as the train pulled away from the little station. He was on the right track to catch up with the Evil One, but now his chase had gotten more intriguing. Why was this shit-eating dog following a man in a buffalo coat?

Then he thought back to the lies he told the station manager. He smiled as he remembered how quick-witted he had been. The lies sounded good as he replayed them in his head. He would have to use them again, and he had plenty of time to embellish his story, if need be.

-27-

fiche a seacht

Black Wolf tracked the Evil One across the Midwest to Chicago. Between every stop he mentally polished and embellished his story about needing to find his partner and his boss so they could rejoin the Wild West Show.

"I've got to catch them so I can apologize for drinking too much and then get back to shooting arrows," he was quick to add if asked why he was trying so hard to find this little man and the tall man traveling with a redheaded woman.

At almost every stop the answers were the same. Sure, someone may have seen them. The skinny little man was here a couple of days, or maybe was it a couple of hours, just missing the tall man and the redheaded woman.

In Chicago, he stored his belongings in a large public locker in Union Station and went in search of the mission where his brother worked. He got off the bus a policeman had told him to take and walked toward the address the cop had given him. As he approached St. Nicholas's Mission, he was shocked at what he saw. Men of all ages and sizes, women with children in tow, lined up on the sidewalk. The line of gaunt and disheveled people stretched around the corner to the front doors of the mission. A woman walked down the line handing out halves of sandwiches to those in line.

"You'll get warm soup when you get inside," she said every 10 feet or so. A child of about 11 ran up to her carrying another basket of sandwiches, and ran back around the corner carrying the empty basket.

"Please be patient," the woman said to no one and to everyone. "There's warm soup and hot coffee inside."

Black Wolf walked slowly past the hungry people to the front doors of the mission. A kindly priest put a hand on Black Wolf's arm.

"Please go to the end of the line, friend."

"I'm here to see my brother," Black Wolf said quietly.

"And who might that be?"

"His name is George Little Bear and he sent word that he works here."

The priest fell silent for a brief moment.

"Please keep moving inside," he said to the people in line and smiled warmly at them. When he turned back to Black Wolf, a tear ran down his cheek.

"I'm sorry," he said, "but we didn't know who to tell. George died two months ago of pneumonia."

"I sent him a coat."

"Yes, and he was so grateful, but he burned the crate it came in to keep the street people warm. He sold the coat, though, to a big Irishman" the priest added, "and then dear George donated all the money to our mission."

Black Wolf's shoulders drooped as he slowly turned away from the priest. As he walked up the street away from the mission doors, he said to people walking by, "He was an old fool … A dumb fucking Indian."

Dazed by his grief and severely disappointed that his much-anticipated reunion with his brother never happened, Black Wolf wandered the streets of Chicago and the shore of Lake Michigan for hours. Eventually, he headed back to Union Station with his head a little clearer, but with a pain in his empty heart. What had started out as joy at the thought of seeing his brother again, had turned into grief and mourning.

Inside the station he sat on a bench in front of his locker while he thought about growing up with his kid brother. He considered abandoning his quest. But memories of the horrors his granddaughter and other innocent Lakota girls had endured at the hands of the Evil One reignited the fire of vengeance in his belly. The warrior bolted straight up, emptied the locker, and resumed his hunt.

As he walked out of the train station, Black Wolf reasoned that if the tall man was trying to escape from somewhere or someone, the best way for him to do that without leaving much of a track to follow would be by boat. Not too many passenger boats on this big lake, so he probably would work on a ship.

Down on the docks, he told the captain of the Washington Lee his much-embellished story about wanting to rejoin Colonel Wood's Wild West Show, which he knew had sailed off to England for a command performance for His Royal Highness George V, who – it was said – was fascinated by the Old West and especially the aborigines who lived there.

"You have any experience working on a ship," the captain asked him.

"No, but I know how to mop a floor," he replied.

The captain looked hard at him. He had never before hired an inexperienced sailor, let alone a fucking Indian, but the old man's story impressed him.

"You carry the buckets and fetch whatever anyone tells you to," he snarled. "Go aboard and head below decks. Someone will point you to your bunk. And stay out of my way!"

Black Wolf picked up his gear and started up the gang plank.

"One more thing," the captain said. Black Wolf turned to look at him. "If you fall overboard, we ain't fishin' for ya."

Black Wolf nodded and headed onto the deck. When he struggled to get his gear below decks, a tall man grabbed the large hat box from him.

"Follow me and I'll show you where you can stow your gear," he said in a thick Irish brogue as he led the way down one passageway and down another ladder.

"You may have to stow the arrows under your bunk," he said when they got to the crew's quarters.

"Much obliged," Black Wolf said. He stared after the man. "Now," he thought to himself, "where's the Evil One?"

-28-

fiche a hocht

Jamestown, North Dakota

Smoke from cheap cigars hung in the hotel lobby like dense fog over a lake. The foul odor mingled with stale perfume and sweat-soaked wool union suits. There also lingered the musty smell of old wood that had repeatedly gotten wet from spring and summer humidity and dried out in the prairie's long, dry winters. Men and women passengers from the stranded train sprawled on the floor. In one corner, a four men played cards crowded together at a small table.

Outside the hotel the blizzard that had started out as a postcard perfect snowfall, raged, the wind howled and made the window frames rattle and vibrate and whistle with irritating irregularity.

The hotel clerk sat on an old bar stool behind the front desk. He rested his chin in his hands and read an old dog-eared copy of National Geographic magazine, staring for the umpteenth time at the black and white photo of a group of bare-breasted African women dancing to the beat of an off-camera drum.

O'Connor and Brigid stood at the counter. Unable to get the clerk's attention, O'Connor put his open hand on the magazine page. The clerk looked up and stared blankly.

"When's the next train, man," O'Connor asked through clenched teeth.

"Won't do ya no good. When the sheriff called to find out if we had food, he said the trains ain't runnin. Tracks covered over. Be days."

Brigid turned away, stepped over three bodies, and stomped up the stairs. The phone rang. The clerk answered it, listened for a few seconds and hung up. He looked out at the motley crew in the lobby, and yelled, "Firemen hitched up an old fire wagon to coupla horses and are bringing us food, folks. They should be here by noon."

People stirred, some looked up, others, bored, stared out the whistling, rattling windows. A woman sitting on the floor in one corner coughed and tried to stop the cigar smoke's assault on her lungs by covering her nose and mouth with a wool scarf. After a minute the scene looked the same as it had for the previous three hours.

O'Connor surveyed the room and turned back to the clerk.

"Lively bunch."

"No sense getting excited over a blizzard. It'll blow over when it's done blowin."

"You otta write a book of philosophy."

The clerk looked at him with a blank expression. O'Connor pulled a silver dollar out of his pocket and threw it to the clerk who caught it with surprising ease.

"Get us when that food comes and I'll throw another dollar yer way."

The clerk nodded and stuck the coin in his pocket. O'Connor turned away, surveyed the scene in the lobby, shook his head in disgust and bewilderment and walked up the stairs.

-29-

FICHE A NAOI

Chicago, Illinois

Clayton Andrews occupied his large custom-made leather chair behind his massive teak desk like a statue. His spine was as rigid as the chair's back, his shoulders were squared off like a Royal Marine standing at attention, which he had been at the turn of the century. His brother, Charles, stood behind him looking out the window of the fourteenth floor of the Pittsfield Building at the skyline of Chicago on New Year's Eve 1930.

Three years earlier, Charles Andrews, Clayton's younger brother, had immigrated to America and joined his brother's firm, which out of loyalty, Clayton renamed Andrews and Andrews. Charles was a wisp of a man, light skinned and with an unruly head of blonde hair, which he daily tamed with copious amounts of pomade in the style of the Roaring Twenties.

"The employees will want to go home early, Clayton."

"Might as well. I'm sure they're not very productive."

Both men turned silent again, lost in different thoughts.

"Will we need to let any more go, Clayton?"

"Not if our Mr. O'Connor does what..."

"For the tenth time, my dear brother, he's not MY Mr. O'Connor. And I didn't want anything to do with him."

"Such a baby still, aren't you Charles? Father was right

… Mother did keep you a little too close to her apron."

"Shut your mouth!"

"Time you finally grew up, my little, little brother. We own a sinking ship. A year ago, we lost our best architect out that very window because he had tried to get rich in the damned stock market. Remember?

"Of course I remember."

"And do you also remember the one-hundred-and-fifty architects, draftsmen and secretaries we turned out three weeks later?"

"Do you have a point, Clayton?"

"For the love of God, grow up! How long do you think we'll keep this firm open designing dime stores and gas stations?"

"But it's steady wor…"

Clayton rose up from his chair and pounded his fists on the desk. The veins on his forehead bulged through the red of his skin.

"Goddamn it, Charles! Steady work slows the blood and the brain! We need a showpiece. Something that will have the Carnegies of the world begging Andrews and Andrews to design their skyscrapers." He breathed deeply and turned to look at his little brother who now faced him.

"Find out if Mr. O'Connor was successful, and if our man or my daughter took care of him."

Charles walked slowly toward the office door. Clayton sat down slowly, swiveled his chair and stared out the window.

Charles turned back to speak.

"Clayton?"

"What is it?"

"Sorry."

"I know, Charles."

Charles quietly turned the door knob, opened the massive door, and sheepishly walked out, shutting the door gently.

Clayton stared out the window at the city he loathed for what it had become, for what he had become. He held his hands together almost as if in prayer and rested his index fingers against his lips. Tears of anger welled up in his eyes.

-30-

TRÍOCHA

Chicago, Illinois

The white-haired man stood alone on the rooftop of an apartment building at the edge of downtown Chicago. He wore a long black overcoat, black leather gloves and a white shirt with a red bow tie. He looked out over the city to the west for a few minutes and turned toward the center of the roof. As he approached a small hut built there, his pigeons cooed. He strode to a small door and opened it.

The man checked the pigeons and then checked their food and water containers. Picking up a bit of food, he held out his hand to the pigeons. Two fed from his hand. As they pecked at his hand, he looked toward an empty arrival pen, then out over the city through the chicken fencing. Sighing, he pulled his hand out of the cage and walked out of the coop, latching the door.

Two hundred miles to the west, a lone pigeon with the red band on its leg fluttered into the open hay loft door at the top of a large round barn. She lit on a rafter among other pigeons and rested next to a large male. She was cold and losing strength, but her training and instincts would not let her quit. Spotting the grain on the barn floor, she glided down and began to peck at the kernels.

-31-

TRÍOCHA A HAON

Jamestown, North Dakota

O'Connor held two pair, the aces and eights of Spades and Clubs, and the Jack of Diamonds. He didn't know it, but it was the infamous dead man's hand drawn by Wild Bill Hickok on August 2, 1876, in Deadwood, Dakota Territory. Brigid had three kings and two jacks, a respectable full house. They had been playing five-card-draw for nearly two hours in their room and were getting bored with the game and with each other.

The only words they spoke were the number of cards they wanted and the bet. There was no sound other than the wind and the rattling of the windows.

"Call."

"Whatcha got, darlin'?"

"Read 'em and weep. Full house." She fanned the cards on the small table between them, snapping them with her thumb.

"You win again," O'Connor sighed in mock resignation, laying down his hand face up. Brigid glanced down at the cards and then looked more closely. She had heard of the hand, but in all her years playing parlor games with her friends and their boyfriends, she had never seen anyone get this exact hand.

Brigid picked up the deck and tapped O'Connor's cards.

"This is the hand Wild Bill Hickok held when he got shot in Deadwood. It means you'll die soon."

"Who was he and am I supposed to worry? I ain't superstitious."

"And you Papists blessing yourselves before you do anything the least bit out of the ordinary isn't superstitious," she chided.

"I do not do that. If I did, I would never get anything done. I would be makin' the sign of the cross constantly. Besides, Miss High and Mighty, it ain't superstition, it's prayin.'"

"Yah, so everyone can see how pious you are."

Brigid rose from the chair and stretched. "My buttocks hurts."

"You are a pain in mine, that's fer sure."

"Remember the Dead Man's Hand," she snorted derisively looking him in the eyes. "I'm going to the lobby. It has to be more exciting than this."

She walked out the door and slammed it shut behind her. O'Connor locked it with the loose deadbolt, then went to the window and stared out, trying to focus on the snow flying by. The attempt hurt his forehead. His brain had been working constantly trying to figure out why his employers had sent this woman to kill him.

He sat on the edge of the bed, untied his hobnail boots and pulled them off. Bored to exhaustion, he lay back on the bed, closed his eyes and immediately fell asleep. His ability to fall asleep quickly and anywhere had served him well in the war and his travels. His ability to awaken even more quickly had saved his life more times than he cared to remember.

In what seemed like only few moments later, O'Connor

heard the soft click of the key in the deadbolt lock. His muscles tensed and he opened his door-side eye a slit. As the door creaked open, the light from the bare bulb in the hallway crept up O'Connor's legs until Brigid's body shielded the bottom rays. He saw the outline of her head and shoulders as she entered fully and closed the door behind her.

"Have any luck findin' another pistol," he asked her. She jumped slightly at the sound of his voice, but quickly regained her composure.

"I thought you were sound asleep," she said.

"I was."

"Seems no one but me carries a weapon in this gawd forsaken state."

"Too bad. I was looking forward to taking another one from you."

Fully awake now, he watched as Brigid sat on her own bed, removed her boots, laid back and rested her head on the pillow. She stared at the dark ceiling.

"Why did you come back up? Why didn't you try to get away with someone?"

"Well, ya stupid Mick, there's a little winter storm raging and, besides, they were all worse poker players than you are."

"So you're growing fond of me, then," he said.

"Like I'm fond of saddle sores!"

O'Connor smiled in the darkness and fell back asleep. Brigid turned her head toward his rhythmic breathing. Killing him would be more difficult to carry out, she thought. Much to her chagrin, she was growing fond of the man she had known in Ireland as a young terrorist rescued by her father.

He had grown from the wounded teenager into a fine

specimen of a man, she thought. She admired his rugged looks, square jaw and slightly bent nose. She could tell by the way the large coat hung on his shoulders and the way he walked that he was in good physical condition, which meant he would not be easy to kill.

The next morning brought more discouragement. Although the blizzard had abated, mountains of snow covered the entire landscape and buried the town. Out their window, O'Connor and Brigid watched as people shoveled snow off their roofs. Some children jumped from the roof of one house into a 12-foot drift and had to be rescued by adults.

Streets were impassible and a deadly chill engulfed the town. Down the street from the hotel, the train depot stood vacant except for the station manager and his dog, which O'Connor could see romping through snow banks on the tracks. His owner struggled to clear snow from the elevated platform, but no trains would move for days.

O'Connor and Brigid headed down the stairs to the hotel lobby. As they went lower, the stench of stale body odor and the collective morning breath of 17 people either unable or unwilling to bother with personal hygiene hit their nostrils. The hotel's night clerk saw no reason to offer his bathroom to any of them, other than for urination. The other business could wait, he thought.

"If someone wants to clear a path to the outhouse, there's a shovel inside by the back door," he announced to the sprawled bodies. No one budged. O'Connor came down the steps just in time to hear the proclamation. Without a word he went back up to his room, pulled on his buffalo great coat, and headed back down the stairs, clomped down the hall and out the back door.

An hour later, cold but invigorated, O'Connor came back into the lobby.

"Ladies and gentlemen, there's now a path to the outhouse," he announced. "And I assure you, the privy works just fine."

Brigid smiled. She had brushed past O'Connor to the hall as he finished his announcement, found an empty chair and claimed it before anyone else could. She picked up a 1923 issue of McClure's Magazine and began to flip through its yellowed pages without really paying attention to its content. O'Connor perched himself five steps up the stairs and stared deep in thought out a window.

As she leisurely reclined, Brigid glanced up and noticed four men huddled in a corner playing cards and talking in whispers. Every now and then, one would look her way then at the staircase. Brigid didn't care what the smelly vermin were talking about or why they were looking at her or O'Connor, so she looked back at her magazine and landed on an article about French corsets.

Brigid was so enthralled by the writer's detailed description of the apparel that women in Europe suffered to wear that she failed to notice the four men standing in a semi circle around her chair. She caught movement out of the corner of her eye when a shadow crossed over the page she was reading. She looked up to see the wild look on all four of the men's faces. Just then one of them grabbed for her left arm, another two went for her legs.

One of the men was near the back of the group. He barked, "Haul 'er out back, boys! We'll all get some fine lovin' today!"

Brigid kicked with all her might to free her right leg and caught the man who had been holding it in the chin with the ball of her foot. He cursed and grabbed her ankle. The three men dragged Brigid kicking a screaming toward the hotel's back door. Everyone else in the room just sat. Some stared, others looked away. The men had her halfway to the door when the man holding Brigid under her arms was suddenly jerked backward and dropped her.

O'Connor let go of the man's shirt collar and hit him in the throat with the second knuckles of his right hand. The man gasped for air and his face turned from red to blue-grey before he passed out, both hands holding his throat.

With her shoulders free, Brigid twisted her body and freed her feet from the men's' grasp. As one of them bent down to regain purchase, O'Connor hit him with all his might on the top of the head. The man's neck cracked loudly and he immediately passed out. The man who had been holding Brigid's other foot put out his arms in surrender. Brigid jumped up, landed on both feet and hit the man with a powerful uppercut that broke his unprotected jaw.

Both O'Connor and Brigid went after the ringleader, but while they stepped over two bodies he hightailed it out the door.

"Let him freeze," O'Connor laughed.

Later in the day, Brigid, O'Connor and the others who could chew were finishing off the sandwiches and pie the firemen had managed to deliver before the streets became impassible. They had scooped snow into every container they could find, including two old spittoons the hotel used as decorations. The melted snow was their only drinking water since the hotel's potable water source was a well just off the back porch which had frozen over within hours of the start of the blizzard.

Until someone could get water and more food to them,

the hotel's guests were going to get hungry, thirsty, and much ornerier.

"I could've taken the bastards," Brigid said to O'Connor between bites.

"I saw you had the situation under control," he laughed.

Later that afternoon, O'Connor lay on his bed reading "The Journal of the World's Greatest Buffalo Hunter," which he had found in the hotel's small bookcase. It was written in the florid language of the late 19th Century, and O'Connor found it slow reading. Nonetheless, the descriptions of buffalo hunts intrigued him.

Brigid was lying on her bed, her face toward the wall. "D'ya think we'll ever get out of here," she asked.

"So you're awake? No, we'll die here of boredom if we don't starve to death first."

"Seriously, Jack."

"Seriously? I would let you eat my arm before I let you starve."

"Oh, never mind." After a minute she quietly said, "Thanks for rescuing me, Jack. I still could've taken them, though."

"Sure thing, darlin'," O'Connor said. Her use of his first name didn't escape him. He had never told her what it was, but he smiled anyway still wondering where they met before he 'rescued' her on a snowy gravel road.

They passed the rest of the day playing cards with others in the hotel lobby. Just before sundown, the clouds lifted and the sky turned a bright blue. O'Connor and a few others cheered.

Nightfall settled in, and the guests who had rooms headed to them. Some of the men still played cards. Cursing was the standard mode of communication in the stuffy room. Brigid walked ahead of O'Connor up the stairs. He had instinctively placed his hand on the small of her back. She didn't jerk away and seemed to welcome his touch by ever so slightly leaning into the palm of his hand.

I've spent far more time with this man than I ever did with the society boys in Chicago, she thought.

When they got to the hotel room door O'Connor reached in front of her and inserted the key in the deadbolt lock. Brigid pushed on his hand while turning the doorknob to open the door. She held her hand there for a brief moment as they entered the room. Her touch broke the barrier between them. O'Connor reached for the light switch and Brigid stopped his hand from turning on the light. She held his hand and turned toward him, lifting her face to kiss him.

O'Connor hesitated. Had she snuck a knife in? Was she trying to kill him again?

Then Brigid put both of her hands behind his neck and pulled him into her warm lips. He didn't resist. Couldn't resist. Being in her presence these past few days, laughing with her, sharing stories about their growing up in different worlds, had brought them closer than many friends could ever become. Their familiarity turned to attraction.

Brigid's hands were suddenly tugging at his belt. He ran his hands around her back and onto her breasts. They tore each other's clothes off, and O'Connor fumbled with her undergarments.

She laughed, unhooked her brassiere strap, pulled off her pantaloons and put her hands on O'Connor's shoulders. His hands cupped her breast and she gasped slightly. He lightly pinched her erect right nipple between the thumb and forefinger of his left hand as he put his right hand on her smooth muscular buttocks. Her tongue explored his mouth.

She ran it over his teeth and darted it along the tip of his tongue and sometimes lightly over his lips.

Wet now, Brigid brought her legs up around his waist. They stood in the embrace for a full minute before O'Connor walked to her bed.

"I am not a hooker, Mick," she said softly. "You don't need to rush."

"Good to know," he laughed.

Afterward, O'Connor lay on his back and Brigid had her head on his flat chest. His hair tickled her cheek. She didn't mind, in fact, she twirled it with her forefinger.

He stroked her side and back for a long time and she breathed evenly, fully relaxed in his arms, and she gasped slightly whenever his hand reached between her legs.

They talked about family. Brigid began to understand the hopelessness of growing up poor Irish under British rule. She knew her life with all its petty problems had been far easier, so much so that hearing him describe his years after his family's tragedy made her embarrassed and a little ashamed. In this moment, though, she was grateful for some of what he had experienced.

Well rested after talking so long, she glided her left hand down his chest toward his groin, stopping along the way to rub his taught lower stomach and then his muscular thighs. She slowly worked her way up.

Without a word, she mounted him, gliding him gently into her. In control, she moved her hips and leaned both hands on his chest. Instinctively, O'Connor gently massaged her breasts. She swayed, ground her hips into him faster. As her body began to quiver, O'Connor suddenly withdrew and pushed her aside.

"What are you doing?" she yelped.

In answer, he gently shoved her onto her back and kissed his way down her body.

"Oh, God!" she moaned, as he worked his tongue on her like a certain whore in Amsterdam had taught him.

When she thought she couldn't stand anymore, he entered her again. A flood of ecstasy almost made her faint as they climaxed together. After a while O'Connor began to withdraw.

"No, stay," she said.

He did. He fell asleep in her arms and legs. A few minutes after O'Connor began to snore softly, Brigid rolled onto her side with O'Connor still in place. She pulled her leg out from underneath him and took a deep breath. This would definitely make killing him more difficult, she thought as she fell asleep with her arm across his flat, muscular chest.

-32-

TRÍOCHA A DÓ

Steele, North Dakota

The Bismarck police chief and the Emmons County sheriff stood in the snow-covered gravel next to the station's lone bubble-top gas pump. They seldom got along and rarely cooperated on catching criminals. As the head policeman in a town that only 50 years ago had been known for gun fights, knife fights, cattle stampedes, and the ugliest prostitutes north of Texas, Chief Thorson took a hard line on criminals.

The county sheriff held the opinion that his only job was to take care of the German immigrants and their property. They may drink too much home-brewed beer at weddings, but for the most part they were strict with their children, had stable marriages, and were kind to their animals. His toughest job was getting re-elected, which meant visiting their farms, most often around dinner time. As a general rule he never rushed to catch Bismarck's fugitives from justice. This was different, though. It had affected his life and the life of his unborn child.

Thorson stood with his right hand on his pistol and his other hand on his hip. He looked west up the road toward Bismarck. The blizzard had finally stopped three days ago and he had been able to ride his horse on the snow-covered highway from Bismarck.

"And before all that, the robber tied you up and just

waited?" It sounded incredulous, he thought.

"Yah."

"How much did he take outta your till, sheriff?"

"Nuddink. I never heard him open the till. Me und Helga figured he didn't think it vas vorth his time."

Thorson turned and looked the man in the eyes.

"How would he know it wasn't worth his time unless he opened your till?"

The sheriff answered with a shrug of his shoulders.

"This here clairvoyant robber never looks in your till but just waits to kill and rob whoever shows up next?"

"Yah."

Thorson stepped forward to the blood spot on the ground, looked down at it and then looked off to the east.

"Show me the body," he said, still looking down the road.

-33-

TRÍOCHA A TRÍ

Jamestown, North Dakota

O'Connor and Brigid circled each other in the middle of the room. They had pushed the beds back against the walls. After several seconds, they began to wrestle. The wrestling continued for several minutes until O'Connor pinned Brigid to the floor. She glared up at him and struggled to get free.

"You're not going to win," he said as he got off.

They sat on the dusty floor, she with arms wrapped around her drawn-up legs, he with his legs outstretched.

"I'm sorry I struck you the first night," he said sincerely.

"And I'm sorry you found my gun," she joked.

Later that evening they stood naked together looking out the room's dirty window at the stars. The night sky was bright from the moon shining off the snow. "We should be able to catch the train east tomorrow," he said. Then he turned and cupped her chin in his hand. She reached her hand up and covered his with a gentle caress.

The next morning the January sun glistened off the mountains of snow that covered the town. People jostled behind them as O'Connor and Brigid waited on the platform for the conductor to call for boarding.

O'Connor was anxious to get out of this sparsely populated country and back to the obscurity of New York. He hated the place, but it was easy to hide there among the other Irish. He promised himself that he would take his $10,000 fee for this last job and return to Ireland. He dreamed for a moment what life would be like there with the money—a farm, sheep, peace. The conductor's yell brought him out of his trance.

"Train to St. Paul, Milwaukee and Chicago. ALL ABOARD!"

The impatient crowd rushed to board the train. They had been holed up in cramped spaces for four days with little sleep, nearly fatal boredom, and the inability to practice their usual personal hygiene. They smelled bad and felt worse, wanting only to depart this prairie village and get on with their lives.

O'Connor walked slowly and deliberately behind Brigid protecting her from the crush of bodies. She put one foot on the train car steps and her foot slipped causing her to fall back. O'Connor caught her and firmly pushed her up. He elbowed a burly fellow behind him who was attempting to board next and climbed on board behind her. The man swung at O'Connor, but the crowd was too close to him for the roundhouse to connect. The man's meaty fist struck the hand rail and he cursed. Not wanting a confrontation, O'Connor didn't look back at him, and he and Brigid entered the passenger car and hurriedly walked down the aisle. When they reached the first two open seats, Brigid slid over to the window seat and O'Connor took the leather bag from her and threw it in the overhead rack. As he slid in beside her she put her arm through his and turned and looked into his eyes.

"I'm certainly glad I tamed the wild Irish beast."

"What makes you think you did?"

"A lady knows."

"So you're a lady now?"

She ignored his tease.

"What about your truck?"

"I gave it to the clerk at the hotel. Wasn't mine, anyway. Truth be known, I stole it," he lied.

Brigid shook her head in mock disgust. "You're nothing more than a common criminal."

"Darlin', ain't nothin' common about this criminal."

He gazed past her at the snow-covered plains of North Dakota. Memories of war, the kills, the whole ugly experience invaded his consciousness as they did with disheartening regularity.

The train clacked along the stiff, frozen tracks through the night. Most of the passengers were asleep; some stared blankly into the night, trying to catch some detail, maybe a yard light from a distant farm, a tree, anything.

O'Connor had finally fallen asleep. His face was covered with sweat and he moaned. The demons were sitting on his chest. Brigid stirred and heard him moan, saw the perspiration on his face. She gently, hesitantly reached up and touched his cheek with her coat sleeve to wipe the sweat running toward his jaw line. Immediately O'Connor grabbed her wrist. "That hurts, Jack," she said in a loud whisper so she wouldn't disturb the other passengers. O'Connor looked at her, wide-eyed, and immediately loosened his grip and held on to her hand. She jerked it away and rubbed her wrist.

"Don't," she said. He shrugged his shoulders, wiped the sweat from his face, and closed his eyes hoping the demons were finished with him for now.

-34-

TRÍOCHA A CEATHAIR

The pigeon flew high in the bright blue sky over the outskirts of Chicago. She flew straight at a group of buildings, circled overhead, and then darted between them as if showing off. Her journey had been long and arduous, filled with danger that nearly ended her life, but she couldn't remember any of it. Her only thought, if pigeons have thoughts, was that she must satisfy the urge deep in her brain to reach her destination. She knew she would be safe, well fed, and coddled by the creature she loved and wanted to please.

After three more joyous circles around the buildings, she spread her wings wide and landed on a wood ledge by the receiving cage and began to coo. The other pigeons in the loft cooed with her. Her long journey over, the little pigeon with the red band entered the loft through a trap door.

-35-

TROChA A CÚIG

Chicago, Illinois

Samuel Phillips sat alone in his well-appointed office furnished richly with dark wood and leather. Odd bronze sculptures on black marble pedestals stood silently around his office like statues in the Roman Forum. Architectural drawings cluttered his desk.

Phillips pored over the drawings on his desk again and again as he dreamed about the fame, and, he hoped, fortune the new building would bring him. Consumed by his daydream, the knock on his office door startled him. He quickly rolled up the plans and shoved them behind the curtain behind his desk.

"Come in."

His longtime secretary, Elizabeth, wearing her signature red dress, entered the office. A large woman with black hair pulled back tightly into a bun at the back of her head, she always wore a red dress because, as she had told him after their first tryst in his office, red went well with her hair.

"Your banker called three times and your lawyer called twice, Sam. It's really getting embarrassing."

"I know, Betsy. Just a few more days."

Elizabeth raised her eyebrows and looked at the ceiling.

"It's your business. But Sam, if you're going under, let the rest of us know so we can look for other jobs."

"Betsy, we're not going out of business. Besides, who'd hire you after you've spent the best fifteen years of your life working for me?"

She walked over to him, leaned over and kissed him full on the lips. "Not even the Rush Street Mission, or my own mother, for that matter." She straightened up, smoothed her dress and left the office closing the door behind her.

Phillips hurried to the closet, took his black cashmere coat off the hanger and slipped it on. Then he walked to a paneled wall and pressed on the head of a sculpture of a hawk with a smaller bird in its claws. The wall opened and Phillips entered the secret passageway. He emerged from another hidden door and into the stairwell. He climbed the narrow stairs to the roof where he cautiously opened the door to the roof and scanned the roofs of nearby buildings. Seeing no one on any of them, he focused his attention on the sky – empty save for a few clouds.

Then, as he had every day for the past week, Phillips walked quickly to the pigeon loft, unlatched the people door, ducked his head and entered. He looked at the entrance cage and then began examining the pigeons, concentrating on their legs. One caught his eye. He slowly reached in with his right arm so he wouldn't set off a flurry of flapping wings and gently wrapped his fingers around the small grey bird with the iridescent green head and the red band around her leg.

"Hello, my darling!" He glanced skyward. "Thank you, Lord."

Phillips removed the red band from the pigeon's leg and examined the body and wings of his champion. When he was satisfied that she was in good condition, he held her up to his face. He pursed his lips and the pigeon lightly pecked at them.

"There's a good girl."

Phillips set the pigeon back on her roost. He reached into his coat pocket and pulled out a small handful of cracked corn, which he held up to her. She pecked at it and cooed. When she had finished eating, he stroked her neck with the back of his right forefinger. At least she was reliable, unlike people.

Phillips closed the cage, and backed out of the roost. Once more he scanned the roofs of adjacent buildings and headed across the roof and went out the exit door, excited by the prospect of building the most singular state capitol in America.

-36-

TRÍOCHA A SÉ

Jamestown, North Dakota

"He'd most probably be taller'n' most," an exasperated Jake Tilden said to the Jamestown depot manager.

"Why's that?"

"'Cause, like I already toldja twice, he could be wearin' a long buffalo hide coat."

"No need to get snippy, young fella."

"Well, did a tall man wearin' a long fur coat get on the train here?"

"Coulda," the station manager said.

Tilden's face turned red with anger, but he took that as a yes.

After Tilden snooped around the North Dakota capitol grounds, he became convinced an arsonist had burned the building to the ground. Standing in the cinders-and-soot-covered muddy slush, he peered down into the smoldering burned-out remains and wondered why, but decided that didn't matter as much as proving to everyone concerned that he was the best goddamned tracker of the 20th Century, even if it was only 1931. His suspicion was confirmed when he got a late night visit at the boarding house from a tall man who introduced himself simply as 'Stratford.'

"We understand you suspect arson in the capital building fire," Stratford said, after gently closing the door to

Tilden's room.

"Yah, so who the fuck are you and why do you care what the fuck I suspect," Tilden said nervously.

"Let's just say I can confirm your suspicion."

"I fucking knew it," Tilden yelled.

"Keep your voice down!"

"So what do you want," Tilden asked.

"The people I represent have an offer for you," Stratford said. "We would prefer that no one else find out the truth. Ever. So what we need you to do …"

Stratford had given Tilden all the details of the fire and the man who set it.

"We've set him up with his family farm in Ireland, so he thinks he's home free. But we don't want him getting comfortable enough that he feels the need to unburden his guilt. We had a man stationed a few miles east, but I just got word from the sheriff that he failed us. We also have a woman positioned as a backup, but no one trusts her to complete the job. You are our insurance if the woman fails us."

"Why me," Tilden asked.

"We know of your, shall we say, special talents."

"What do you want me to do?"

"We want you to follow the tall Irishman and unburden him … permanently. If you kill him before he gets to Ireland, all the better. When you've succeeded, send a telegram to me in Chicago at the address written on a slip of paper inside your stack of money. I'll wire you another $10,000."

Stratford had given Tilden $10,000 'for expenses of your trip' he had said.

"How will you know I actually succeeded?"

"Don't worry, Mr. Tilden, I'll know."

"Agreed?" Stratford asked.

"When do I fucking start," Tilden said, pacing excitedly in his room.

"Leave tomorrow. He's already got a three-days head start," Stratford said as he opened the room's narrow door. "Don't disappoint me, Mr. Tilden. I don't like people to disappoint me."

With that, he walked out and quietly closed the door.

The following day, his belly burning with the thrill of the chase, Tilden had boarded the eastbound train in Mandan hoping to catch up to the man who had pulled off the crime and gotten away. He would dispatch the Irishman quickly, but if any woman was with him, he would have some fun with her then kill her slowly, savoring her suffering.

He had been antsy on the ride from Mandan, pacing up and down the aisle, falling onto the occasional seated passenger whenever the train lurched one way or the other. It had sped up many times to plow through snow drifts across the tracks. The lurching when the train hit the drifts pissed him off the most, but it meant getting to the next stop quicker, so he accepted each temporary inconvenience.

When the train stopped in Jamestown to take on supplies, a new crew, and for the yard crew to knock ice from the train's engine wheels, Tilden got off to snoop around. While the other passengers got off because it was their destination, he had stood in a corner and studied the passengers waiting to board. He stared at each one, looking for some detail, a large bundle tied with rawhide that could hold a buffalo coat, anything that looked suspicious. His stares made the others uncomfortable. The women diverted their eyes, some of the men glared back at him, but Tilden didn't care. He was a tracker, a Pinkerton agent, not a gentleman.

Seeing nothing his trained eyes could detect as guilt, he went to the ticket office and began questioning the station manager, somewhat nonchalantly at first, but becoming impatient at the old man's density. Finally getting the man to admit that a tall man could have been a passenger in the past couple of days rekindled the fire in Tilden's belly. His palms began to sweat at what else the man had told him. "Maybe had a redheaded gal with him," the man volunteered. "Couldn't be sure, though."

Now, at each depot, he would ask about a tall man traveling with a redheaded woman. This major clue thrilled Tilden beyond his ability to contain his joy. When he stepped on the first rung of the metal step on the passenger car, he could no longer contain himself and let out a whoop that quickly evolved into a guttural holler.

At each depot down the line, Tilden's routine was the same. He slowly scanned the waiting room, staring longingly whenever he spied a young girl or woman traveling alone. Then he would remind himself that he was on a mission and would have more time to enjoy the finer things they had to offer once he completed his task and was again riding high. When no travelers matched his prey, he would ask ticket agents and porters if they had seen a tall man in a long fur coat accompanied by a redheaded woman.

Their answers were always negative ... until he reached Chicago, a town he knew like an old cougar knows its territory.

"So, you're sure," Tilden pressed the porter.

"Yassuh, like I done said, I offered to carry her bags to the taxi, but the man in the long coat just brushed me aside. He wadn't rude or nothin', and after he put the redhead inta the taxi, he come back and gave me this here gold coin!"

Later, filled with confidence and the thrill of the chase, Tilden checked himself into a modest-looking hotel on Rush Street and spent the next 13 days stalking his prey. He asked at flop houses and fancy hotels about a tall man wearing a buffalo coat; about a redheaded woman alone; about the two of them together. No luck.

At night, he boldly talked his way into speakeasies, but in those he got silent stares and menacing looks. "Why you asking so many questions, short stuff," one large bouncer asked, looking down on him. "The man owes me money," was all Tilden said before he stormed out.

On his fourth full day in Chicago, Tilden began looking in places a tall man with little or no education might find work. He knew enough about Chicago to know that it was the site of major shipping traffic, so Tilden began his daytime hunt on the docks and shipyards. He concocted a story about searching for the man who had hired on at the family farm and had repaid his dear sickly widowed mother for her kindness by stealing her meager life savings from the tin can she kept it in under a board on the porch. "So you can understand why me and my sisters want to find him and bring him to justice," he would say, feigning anger.

In reality Tilden never knew his mother. Shortly after his birth, she had left him with her brother and his sadistic wife, both of whom gave solid meaning to the "spare the rod and spoil the child" method of childrearing. Between the beatings for whatever contrived wrong he had committed, not even the woman ever showed him a lick of affection, preferring instead to allow her own daughters to tickle him mercilessly until he wet his pants. That gave them sheer delight and earned him a severe whipping and a day of no pants or underwear while the only pair of either that he owned dried on the clothesline after he washed them and the woman twisted his ear.

By the time he was 12, Jake Tilden had had enough. One day after school, he just walked the opposite way from home and never looked back. He had learned to hate women, to distrust men and, most importantly over the past few years, to lie well enough to avoid punishment.

As he wandered around, a lone kid eating out of garbage cans and hiding from the cops, he developed the skill of being charming and likable to a person's face and cursing them behind their back. That deception came in handy because he could convince anyone to buy anything from him and believe anything he told them about himself. It also gave him the ability to find people who were gullible enough to believe his lies. Those attributes got his foot in the door at Pinkerton Detective Agency. Tilden told them he attended a small college in Canada that had, unfortunately and to the dismay of everyone who had attended there, burned to the ground after its single building was struck by lightning. And no, he did NOT have any proof that he had graduated from there because the college's records had been turned to ashes in the conflagration. However, he was sure its mother university, Cambridge in England, might have duplicate records if they cared to inquire. They didn't care enough.

So at the ripe old age of 23, a scrappy, wiry Jake Tilden, con artist and polished prevaricator, became a rookie agent for the Pinkerton Detective Agency headquartered in Chicago. He learned all he could by asking questions of his superiors to the point of annoyance.

During physical training, Tilden ran faster and shot better than most. When sparring, he dodged and weaved so quickly that his opponents rarely connected and he fought with such fury and meanness that soon the only opponent he could get was a large punching bag.

At day's end, Tilden would go home, clean up, re-iron one of his signature starched white shirts, and go out for dinner. Alone. That allowed him to prowl the streets hunting his young female prey without having to explain anything to anyone.

He became one of Pinkerton's best, most persistent, and some would later say, most ruthless detectives. He learned what questions to ask about the criminals he tracked and who to ask. He just intuitively knew how to get his man.

When the Northern Pacific Railroad asked Pinkerton to assign a good agent to work its Minneapolis to Bismarck line, management saw the opportunity to rid themselves of a festering problem. They knew about Agent Jake Tilden's proclivities for roughing up young prostitutes and that it would eventually cast aspersions on their organization, so they gave him a $500 bonus to take the job. Two days after he left Chicago for Minneapolis, they congratulated themselves for their stroke of genius and toasted their good fortune at their usual speakeasy.

All went well until they received word of Tilden screwing up after assigning him to help the U.S. Secret Service track down a gang of counterfeiters. Losing a big government contract gave Pinkerton all the excuse they needed to terminate Tilden. They were angry as hell, but relieved to be rid of him.

-37-

TRÍOCHA SEACHT

Chicago's Union Station was as grand a train depot as had ever been built. Popular architect Daniel Burnham had done the original design, and the firm of Graham, Anderson, Probst and White had overseen its completion in 1925.

O'Connor and Brigid stood in the middle of the six-year-old grand hall. Passengers rushed around them, heading anywhere and nowhere. Many were dirt farmers from the South who had spent what egg money they could scrape together to travel to Chicago in hopes of landing a job in the stockyards and slaughterhouses.

Most of the men were disappointed but too dumb to know they were lucky to miss working 12-hour days at violent, demeaning jobs like slugging bellowing cattle in the temples or scraping bloody guts into a waste pit. The women could usually find work sewing tarps for the Great Lakes shipping trade, taking care of other women's children—or taking care of other women's men.

They stood in the center of the massive room and Brigid watched O'Connor gawk at the granite and marble walls and columns. He had never been able to just look at its magnificence, preferring instead to avoid public places in favor of quickly heading to the tracks to board his trains. He also enjoyed watching people when he knew they weren't out to kill him.

"You're staring at people again," Brigid said as she tugged

on his coat sleeve to get his attention. "O'Connor, my father knows people. He can get you a job."

"I can get one."

"But slaughtering cattle! It's so… so violent and menial."

"No shame in hard work, Lass. Let's get you a cab."

They walked up the steps to the main entrance. O'Connor hailed a cab and helped Brigid into the back seat as the driver threw her bag in the seat beside her. She pulled O'Connor to her and kissed him warmly. "We'll see each other soon, Mick," she said throatily.

She let go of his collar and motioned to the driver to go. O'Connor waved slightly and watched as Brigid's cab turned a corner. He went back into Union Station. O'Connor clomped down the steps inside and walked over to a bank of wall phones. He went to the phone nearest the entrance to the trains, lifted the receiver, looked around, inserted two coins and dialed the number he had memorized before burning the slip of paper Stratford had written it on.

As O'Connor waited, he turned around and slowly surveyed the large lobby. People rushed in all directions. Negro porters carted bags on large wheeled carts. A garbled voice barked on the public address system.

Hearing the voice on the other end of the phone, he quickly turned to face the wall.

"Andrews. It's Jack O'Connor . I'm here in Chicago." He listened for a few seconds, anger stirring in him.

"Jaysus, yes it burned! Read the bloody paper. I'm coming over."

The voice interrupted him.

"No, NOW!" O'Connor hissed loudly into the phone.

Composing himself, he hung up the earpiece, looked around again, and headed out the massive front doors.

O'Connor turned left on the street and headed toward the river. He crossed a footbridge, crossed two more streets and entered a tall office building.

In the back seat of the taxi, Brigid nervously chewed her fingernails. Unable to think of the right thing to say, she let the driver continue through unknown streets. Finally reaching a decision, she reached up and tapped the driver on the shoulder. "There. Over there. Let me off at that corner."

The cab pulled over to the curb and Brigid handed the driver a five dollar bill. He started to give her change.

"Keep it," she said as she grabbed her bag and got out of the cab.

Brigid weaved through the people walking on the sidewalk and got in a phone booth on the street corner. She picked up the earpiece then replaced it in the cradle. Three times. Tears welled up in her eyes. Finally, she grabbed the earpiece and quickly dialed the phone.

"Margaret, hello. It's Brigid. Is my father in?"

Brigid looked out of the phone booth, watching the crowd.

"Hello, Father," she said staccato. "I couldn't do it – I didn't know at first if he was the right one then he took the gun away and we were stuck in some horrible snow storm and I never had another chance 'cause he had the gun. And …"

She listened.

"What! You know already?"

There was a long pause.

"You ARE going to pay him, aren't you?"

Another pause.

"No, I don't want to come to your office!"

Brigid hung up the ear piece and screamed in frustration.

She opened the phone booth door and looked around to see if anyone had heard her scream. People rushed by hurrying nowhere. Brigid Andrews walked into the stream of bodies and melted into the crowd.

tríocha a hocht

Samuel Phillips paced as far as the telephone cord would allow. He had come up with this part of his plan in a moment of alcohol-inspired genius the evening prior in his favorite leather chair in his study at home just before his head lowered to his chest and he passed out after his fourth tumbler of Canadian whiskey.

"Look, Inspector, don't ask me how I know. Let's just say a little birdie told me."

On the other end of the telephone call, Inspector Eamon O'Reilly, a slightly overweight man in his early forties with a handlebar moustache, hung up the phone. He talked across two desks facing each other to his partner, Inspector Lou Hargrove, a slim, hard-faced man in his mid-thirties.

O'Reilly wore a rumpled white shirt with a wide-striped neck tie and shiny wrinkled trousers that made him look like he slept in his clothes. Hargrove dressed in a crisply ironed shirt, a red bow tie, and his trousers were neatly pressed by the White Lotus Chinese Laundry on the main floor next to his apartment building. Each detective wore a .45 ACP in a shoulder holster. They preferred the fire power and magazine capacity of the .45 over the standard-issue revolvers carried by uniformed Chicago police.

"Barney Google there says I can meet the arsonist who burned down the capital building in Bismarck, South Dakota," O'Reilly said in his thick Irish brogue.

"I think you mean North Dakota," Hargrove corrected.

"Yeah? You sure? Anyway, says if I go to the office of Andrews and Andrews Architects, I'll be a hero."

"Think we should check it out?"

"'Suppose," O'Reilly sighed. "Gotta be more exciting than this feckin' paperwork."

O'Reilly grabbed a tattered overcoat and Hargrove a silky cream-colored cashmere coat. Heading out of the squad room, they looked like Mutt and Jeff in the comics, but with more fire power.

-39-

TRÍOCHA A NAOI

Clayton Andrews' secretary, Margaret, sat at her desk chewing Black Jack. She liked snapping it because it irritated her boss and anyone who ever came within hearing distance. The licorice also covered up the odor of her breath she got from the roll-your-owns she snuck on the fire escape.

O'Connor opened the outer office door and strode quickly to Andrews' office door. Margaret got up quickly, swallowed her gum in a quiet gulp and ran after him.

"He just barged right in, Mr. Andrews. I had no ti..."

"It's alright, Margaret."

"Should I call the police?"

"No, Margaret. I know Mr. O'Connor. We'll be just fine. Why don't you go to the Building Inspector's Office and scare us up a copy of the building permit on that new school we designed?"

"Yes, sir." Margaret glared at O'Connor and left. Andrews stood and walked around his desk to face O'Connor. "What are you trying to do, get us both arrested?"

"You're talking like I care what happens to the likes of you, you feckin' Brit! I don't. I'll just be taking my money and leaving."

"It's beside the chair."

Andrews pointed to a small leather suitcase sitting beside an overstuffed chair off to one side in front of his desk. O'Connor walked over and sat in the chair. Andrews sat down and eased open a side drawer, watching O'Connor the entire time. He slowly pulled out a derringer and held it in his lap.

"Your gold coins were a stupid idea. All them Krauts in Dakota acted like they'd never seen 'em before."

O'Connor opened the suitcase and peered at the stacks of English Pounds. Satisfied, he began to unpack the money and put it in his coat pockets. He stopped and stared at Andrews, a flash of recognition in his mind. "That was your plan, wasn't it, Andrews? Have me leave a trail of gold coins!"

Andrews ignored the accusation. "Tell me about the fire, Jack."

O'Connor resumed shoving money in his coat, only faster, with more urgency.

"Dry as tinder. It was too easy, though. Some stooge left a bunch of rags in a closet. Mustuv been oiling down all that shiny wood to keep it from cracking. They'll never know."

"Did you enjoy burning down that building, Jack?"

"It was an ugly buildin'."

"How do I know it burned to the ground?"

O'Connor looked at Andrews. He sensed something was going to happen. Slowly he put the last wad of money into an inner pocket toward the rear of his coat where he left his hand.

"Now surely a fancy architect reads the paper. And if you didn't think it was ashes, why'd you get the money ready?"

"Andrews pulled up the derringer and aimed it at O'Connor. Just then, Brigid burst into the room. "Father, NO!"

O'Connor stared at her wide-eyed and jumped up from the chair.

"Well, well," Andrews said to his daughter. "If it isn't my

spineless offspring. If you'd have done what I sent you to do–what you promised me you'd do–Mr. O'Connor would be a frozen stiff right now instead of a problem."

O'Connor looked at her. He finally recognized her. "Brigid! Brigid Andrews? Your own father sent you to kill me! And all along I thought you were just trying to rob me and steal me truck. How could I have been so blind? You British sympathizing whore! The curse of Cromwell on both of ya."

"Jack, I fell in ..." she choked, tears running down her cheeks.

O'Connor, still facing Brigid, pulled his knife from behind his back, wheeled around and threw it. Clayton Andrews leaned sharply to his right and the knife struck him in his left bicep instead of his heart. He dropped the gun, which discharged as it hit the floor, sending a bullet into the nose of a statue of Julius Caesar. Just then, Detectives O'Reilly and Hargrove rushed in, guns drawn, both pointed at O'Connor's chest. He froze, staring at Brigid. Her deceit sucked the fight out of him and for the first time in his life he surrendered peacefully.

-40-

ὀаıсһеаὀ

Two hours later, O'Connor paced inside a large holding cell that was occupied by several other men. His buffalo fur coat lay folded neatly in a back corner of the cell. He stopped pacing long enough to press his right cheek hard between two bars and look as far down the long corridor as he could see. A scruffy bum wearing tattered trousers and a ragged suit coat bent down and stroked O'Connor's coat.

"How's a dumb fuckin' Mick get such a grand coat?" he snorted to the room. O'Connor turned toward the man. The bars had left an impression of his face, but the white of it quickly turned red. "If you touch me coat again, I'll rip out your heart," he said matter-of-factly. The ragged man rose from the metal bench. The other men in the cell crowded around him. They walked en masse toward O'Connor, like a pack of timber wolves approaching a wounded moose. A guard's jingling keys stopped them. Keys clanking and boots clomping, O'Reilly came into view behind the guard. The guard unlocked the cell door and motioned to O'Connor.

"'C'mon, Mick. Grab your coat. You're going for a ride," O'Reilly said.

O'Connor defiantly bumped his way through three men standing in the middle of the cell, picked up his coat from the corner, and walked toward the guard and O'Reilly. He walked out of the cell and the guard closed and locked the door. O'Connor, O'Reilly and the guard walked down the corridor. As they disappeared, the scruffy man thrust his arm out of the bars and stuck up his middle finger in defiance.

In a dark alley behind the police station, O'Reilly and O'Connor stood beside a pile of wood pallets. A light snow fell and the lone street light at the end of the alley gave the scene an eerily peaceful appearance.

O'Connor faced O'Reilly. "So you're going to shoot me here in this place? What happened to American justice?" O'Reilly reached into his pocket. O'Connor braced himself to fight, but instead of a small caliber throw-away pistol, the cop pulled out a long brown envelope. He handed it to O'Connor who opened the envelope and thumbed the large stack of British Pounds.

"Imagine, a Chicago cop on the take," O'Connor smirked.

"Not today. This is the money you had when we brought you in. Can you count, Mick?" O'Reilly asked.

"Can you squeal like a pig?

O'Reilly ignored both insults. He put his gloved hands in his coat pockets and talked to O'Connor like a headmaster would talk to a student he was expelling.

"I know all about you, lad. And the people who are paying us both have booked passage for you on the Washington Lee. It leaves from the Chicago Pier for Canada in two hours. You're smart, you can find your way home from there."

"Home?" O'Connor cried out. "I've got no home!"

"You do, Jack," O'Reilly said soothingly. "Stratford convinced a certain British bank it was in their best interests to give you full title to your farm and to throw in some operating capital, seeing you're a war hero and all. Oh, and a rather large flock of sheep.

Stunned, O'Connor looked up and down the alley, half expecting the cop's accomplice to come around the corner and shoot him. He looked at O'Reilly. "That wasn't part of the deal. What's the catch?"

"Let's just say it's a bonus for a job well done," O'Reilly explained as he reached behind a large crate and withdrew a pigeon in a small cage, which he handed to O'Connor.

"When you get to Canada, throw this wee creature into the air. She'll fly home and Stratford will know you're safe."

"One more thing, Mick." O'Reilly reached into his coat and withdrew O'Connor's knife and handed it to him.

"Now, go," he said. "Some of us should go back to the old sod." Then he added, "If you're still slinkin' around Chicago in the mornin', you'll never see home again."

O'Connor stuffed the envelope in his coat and put the knife inside his belt at the small of his back. He turned and quickly walked past the cop toward the mouth of the alley.

"The rags were brilliant," O'Reilly said to him. O'Connor stopped. He turned around slowly.

O'Reilly continued. "That's the official word, doncha know. Oily rags just went and burst into flames on their own. Just brilliant!"

"It was an ugly buildin'. It deserved to burn," O'Connor said. O'Reilly laughed. O'Connor turned and hurried out of the alley carrying the pigeon. O'Reilly laughed harder and louder. He laughed so hard he had to lean against the side of a building to steady himself. His laughter echoed through the alley and the empty streets. O'Connor started to laugh and then sprinted out of the alley carrying the small pigeon crate. At that hour, he ran through a deserted downtown Chicago toward the pier.

-41-

Daichead a haon

The *Washington Lee* was one of the last operating steamships on the Great Lakes. It sat low in the water now as it took on its cargo of crushed granite for delivery in Montreal. At 927 feet long, it wasn't the largest ship in the company's fleet, but she was a grand vessel and her three 12-man crews and two captains kept her earning money for the CanAm Steamship Company seven days a week, 24 hours a day.

Today was no different. While she seldom took on passengers, her captain, an experienced maritime commander who looked the part with his brown forehead and cheeks hidden by a snow-white beard and moustache, had agreed, with the help of five-hundred pounds British Sterling, to transport an Irishman. He hadn't asked questions, and had told his friend Stratford that it would be no pleasure cruise. The man was to stay out of sight as much as possible, would be fed once a day in his berth near the engine room, and was to talk to no one, especially not the deck hands who had a penchant for scuttlebutt on and off the ship, most often fueled by rum. Sailors loved gossip and the captain did not want tall tales and low morale interfering with the quick delivery of his cargo.

Of course, Stratford had not told any of this to O'Reilly, who had not given any instructions to O'Connor. When he boarded carrying the pigeon, a small knap sack and whistling an Irish jig he had asked several sailors where he could find the captain.

On the bridge, the captain had been more than a little angered by O'Connor's brazenness, but as an experienced captain he had dealt with his share of men with false bravado. However, this man carried himself with the confidence of someone who had survived the worst life had to offer and had become stronger for it.

He didn't know anything about this Irishman other than he was to be given safe passage and was to debark in Montreal.

"You're to stay away from my crew," he had told O'Connor. "If anyone asks, you are the nephew of the owner of the CanAm Steamship Company and you are aboard to determine if you want to work for the company. That will make them avoid you." O'Connor nodded and stepped out of the bridge in search of the engine room.

The old Lakota was swabbing the outer passageway. He tilted his head slightly to the side and watched O'Connor saunter by.

The Indian had signed on as a boiler tender and deck hand telling the ship's first mate he needed to rejoin Texas Jack's Wild West Show, which he claimed was thrilling British royalty in London. The troupe didn't exist, but the old Lakota had shown up wearing a chief's war bonnet and carrying a long, fringed deerskin case, which he told the quartermaster contained his bow and arrows.

The three-day trip to Montreal was without incident, save for a small squall as they entered Lake Erie, which O'Connor had found exhilarating thanks to an "invitation" from the captain to strap himself into the crow's nest atop the signal tower and ride out the storm there. The first mate had suggested it to the captain as a way to entertain the crew and bring the arrogant Mick down a peg or two. He and the captain had laughed at the thought of a landlubber sitting on a small perch at the ship's highest point. Being such, it would sway the widest and the motion often caused hardened sailors to turn green with seasickness. O'Connor surprised the captain by accepting the invitation, and had dumbfounded the crew by not vomiting. He had learned years before early in his passage aboard a British troop transport from England to France in 1918 to keep his eyes on the horizon and let his body sway with the ship during heavy seas.

As the steamship pulled into port, O'Connor leaned on the brass railing at the stern, winter's wind blowing through his hair. His memories of Brigid flooded his mind without warning, and now he allowed himself to become agitated. He pounded his fists repeatedly on the railing berating himself for the hundredth time for being duped by a pretty face. Rage was a rare pleasure, and after a few minutes he made it subside. He stopped pounding on the railing and gripped it hard until his knuckles turned white. He looked east off the ship's starboard side at the rising sun. As it rose higher, its rays washed over O'Connor's face, warming and calming him. His expression changed as he realized that he was, indeed, going home. He would make his way to someplace called Nova Scotia where he hoped to book first-class passage to Ireland on the grandest ship he could find.

O'Connor bent down and lifted the small pigeon cage. He opened the door and pulled out the bird, a yellow band on its leg. Holding the bird gently, O'Connor reached into a coat pocket with his free hand, withdrew a handful of seeds and fed the bird. As the bird ate, O'Connor stroked its feathers. After a while, he held the bird up and looked into its face. Abruptly, O'Connor threw the cooing pigeon into the air and watched it circle the ship and fly away from the rising sun, away from Ireland.

-42-

Daichead a Dói

The ship's pitch and yaw woke O'Connor from a fitful sleep. His nose barely missed scraping the bottom of the bunk above him as he lay on his back, the only position he could take, unless he crawled into the sack face down. He laid there for a few minutes, hoping to fall back asleep, but consciousness seeped back in and he realized sleep this night was over.

He had been forced to book passage as a deck hand on this freighter because it was the only ship heading to Ireland in the next two weeks, and O'Connor desperately wanted to get home and begin his new life.

The captain had wanted to take the northern route from Canada around the tip of Greenland passed Iceland and then to the Arctic Circle, but the first mate reminded him that they had only taken on enough fuel to sail southeast in a straight line to Ireland. The captain had never crossed the Arctic Circle, so he had wanted to be able to brag about crossing the 66° 33' 44" Parallel. Fear for his life and his job, however, meant he and his crew would not be Blue Noses this trip. The North Atlantic was, however, cold enough, to turn exposed body parts blue.

O'Connor grasped the frame of the bunk above him, being careful to not jiggle it so as to awaken the deck ape snoring in it, and slid his six-foot-four-inch frame out of the tight space. He slipped on his boots and reached under his bunk, felt for the buffalo coat. He stood up, quietly lifted the latch on the cabin's bulkhead hatch, and stepped through, ducking as he did. Once in the passageway, he stretched to his full height. Almost. He still had to bend his neck to stand, so he bent his knees and donned the heavy buffalo coat, latching the leather loops over the deer antler buttons as he walked, pressing his right elbow against the bulkhead for stability.

O'Connor climbed ladders up two decks to reach the main deck. As he unlatched the rubber-ringed sea hatch, icy spray caught him square in the face. He was fully awake now. Once he turned his back to the North Atlantic, it took all his strength to close and latch the hatch. O'Connor grasped the railing with his right hand and worked his way aft toward the ship's stern. As he approached, he saw a lone figure standing at the aft rail. The man appeared to be looking for something on the early morning horizon.

When O'Connor approached him, the man didn't turn, but merely shouted above the sound of the waves crashing against the ship, "Nice buffalo coat!"

"How did you know I had on a coat," O'Connor yelled.

"Your boots gave you away, white eyes," the man yelled. O'Connor stood next to the old man, both holding firm to the railing. They stood in silence, taking in the power of the ocean and how insignificant the ship was in the middle of its vastness. After several minutes, the smaller man faced O'Connor, who recognized him immediately.

"Top of the mornin', chief," he shouted. Gettin' ready to put on another show?"

"Not in this wind," Black Wolf shouted back. "'Couldn't hit the side of this big boat."

To maintain his ruse as the star of an Old West Show,

the old Lakota had been forced to use his shooting skills to hit plates thrown over the side by the captain to entertain the crew. The captain had initially demanded that Black Wolf use his bow and arrows, but Black wolf had claimed that the boss of the show had confiscated most of his arrows and taken them with as a way to make the Indian rejoin the troupe when he sobered up. Of course, there were no purloined arrows and Black Wolf never needed to sober up, but he had to concoct more details of his story as he went along. Luckily, he was a sharpshooter in real life, so putting on a show was easy after he got used to the rolling of the ship. The captain had loaned him his ancient Winchester 73, which he kept well oiled and ready to shoot any sharks that ventured close to the ship.

"You're a damn fine shot," O'Connor shouted too loudly. In the time the two had stood at the ship's stern, the sun had peaked up behind them turning the sky red and the sea had calmed.

""I am," said the Lakota, matter-of-factly. "Where'd you get that coat?"

"Bought it off an Indian in America," O'Connor said. "Why?"

Black Wolf turned back to the sea. "I made a coat like that a few years ago and sent it to my brother in a place called Chicago."

"That's where I bought it," O'Connor confirmed.

"I shot the animal then my woman scraped the hide and we made the coat. That coat, I think. Can I look inside?"

O'Connor unfastened the loops over the antlers and opened the coat, exposing the lining.

"Take it off," Black Wolf said.

He didn't know why he did, but O'Connor took off the

coat. With the calm seas, it wasn't as cold as before.

"The old Lakota held open the coat. "You see the wide strip of beads along the middle of the back? That's my mark. Says I made the coat. This buffalo was a proud, lonely bull. He was dying, and I helped him get to the place Tatanka go after they serve my people."

The two men looked silently at each other.

"Did the coat serve you well, white eyes?"

"Aye, it did," O'Connor answered.

With that, the old Lakota twirled around away from O'Connor and flung the coat into the ocean where it landed fur side up. "Now Tatanka is truly free to join his ancestors," he said as he looked into O'Connor's eyes. "And you are free to live your life."

O'Connor stared at Black Wolf and then looked at the coat floating on the prop wash, moving farther away. As he watched, the coat gently slipped beneath the surface once it floated onto the ship's wake. When it disappeared, O'Connor suddenly felt as if a burden had been lifted from his shoulders. He turned to thank the Indian, but he was gone.

-43-

Daichead a trí

O'Connor stood on the ship's bow and breathed the delicious sea air mixed with the unmistakable earthy aroma of Ireland. He would soon be home, but to collect his pay he had much work to do once the ship docked in Limerick. Freight had to be offloaded, decks swabbed, brass polished, lines repaired.

Four days after docking, the ship was ready to take on new cargo to transport to Morocco and from there to New York in America.

"You're a good hand," the captain said to O'Connor as the bursar handed him his pay. "Sure you won't stay on and see exotic ports and their exotic women?"

"Thank you, sir," O'Connor replied, stuffing his money in a front pocket and slinging his sea bag over his shoulder. "I've had enough of the sea for a lifetime. Now it's time to put aside adventure and live the calm life of an Irish shepherd."

"Good luck," the captain shouted as O'Connor tromped down the gangplank. "If you get bored, you're always welcome on my crew."

O'Connor didn't look back. He just stuck his right hand in the air and waved as he walked off the pier headed toward the city.

The old Lakota watched O'Connor from the forecastle. He would have to follow the big white man because he felt the skinny demon wouldn't be far behind.

When O'Connor had turned the corner and could no longer be seen from the ship, Black Wolf gathered his belongings and climbed down to the bursar's table at the head of the gang plank.

"Good luck, old man," the captain said. "Hope you find that Wild West Show before you run out of money."

"I'm a good tracker," Black Wolf said sarcastically.

"No doubt you are," the captain smiled. "Don't shoot yourself in the foot with that pea shooter."

"Thanks for the advice," Black Wolf replied, a little too earnestly. Under his breath he said, "Stupid white man." Then he slung his buckskin bag containing his Sharps over his neck and chest and walked as fast as he could around the corner where O'Connor had disappeared. He caught sight of the man's large frame heading down a street that would take him south into the countryside.

Just how long he would have to follow him before that little white demon showed up he could only guess. It would turn out to be two months.

-44-

Daichead a ceathair

O'Connor walked for four days and three nights. He was lucky to find inns and taverns where he could rest and dream about owning his family farm. He used cash to buy meals and rooms for the night, which gave him a sense of well being. He vowed he would not touch the money he had sold his soul to earn.

At noon on the fourth day, O'Connor walked over a rise on the road and there, spread before him, was the most wonderful, deplorable sight he had seen in many years. His family farm, run down but beautiful, the cottage in disrepair, and with no one to repair it the barn stood ravaged by wind and rain. Undaunted, O'Connor entered the yard, took stock of what needed to be done once the place was his. He glanced up at the hillside with its hidden graves as he walked to the house and pushed open the door that hung on two of the four hinges. The place hadn't been touched in the fifteen years he had been gone, a fact that he was happy to see. It meant there were no squatters. After tossing his bag into the dilapidated bedroom, O'Connor headed to the village and the Land Office.

"What makes you think you can waltz in here and buy a piece of land," the Land Agent, a scrawny middle-aged man wearing his thinning black hair slicked down on his pale white scalp and an even slicker officious look.

O'Connor pulled his British Army discharge paper from

his inside breast pocket, unfolded it and handed it to the bureaucrat, who reluctantly took it.

"What's this, then," he asked looking at the crinkled paper.

"I know the law," O'Connor said. "'Says that I fought in the war for the Brits and Yanks, so I can own land in Ireland. This paper proves that."

"I don't need the likes of you to tell me the law," the land official sniped. He slowly got up and shuffled to the window. He held O'Connor's discharge paper up to the sunlight, turned it flat so he could see the impression of the seal on the Army colonel's name who had signed the discharge that read that O'Connor had "served with distinction and honor and is accorded all the rights and privileges of a faithful veteran of the crown's army."

"Looks legitimate," the bureaucrat said as he slowly sat down. "But how do I know it's not a fake?"

"Want me to show you how I slit the throats of German soldiers," O'Connor asked the man while staring into his eyes.

The land agent coughed and blinked his eyes, which he diverted to a log book on his desk. "What's the description of the land you want to buy?"

"The Paddy O'Connor place," he said.

The man froze. "He was a traitor and so was his whole family," he said, his voice shaking. "That place is off the market."

"Well, now it ain't," O'Connor said. "He was my pa, and I'm claiming it as is my right to do as a war veteran."

The man recomposed himself and read a notation by the land description. "I can't sell it to you," the man said, a look of recognition coming over his face. "Seems you already own it."

At that, he swiveled his chair so he faced the safe behind his desk and spun the combination dial right, left, right, pulled down the handle, opened the safe, reached in and brought out a folded document, which he placed on the desk blotter, and a small leather and brass portfolio, which he thrust at O'Connor.

"I don't know how much is in here, but you're to have it," he said. "A man from a bank in London dropped it off a month ago with instructions for the deed. I didn't know if or when you would show up, so I haven't prepared your deed. It's late," the man complained. "I'll have to do it in the morning."

"You'll do it now," O'Connor demanded. "It ain't that late. I'll wait."

The land agent reached in the top desk drawer and drew out a thick piece of paper that had been made to look like parchment. He unfolded the document on his desk, read it carefully, and then began to transcribe the property description onto the deed in which the British government vested the property in …

"What's your full name, Mr. O'Connor?"

"Jack Paidrig O'Connor. Want me to spell it for you?"

"Won't be necessary." I already know what it is you stupid mick. When you die … soon … your farm goes back to his majesty, the king, according to Stratford's letter.

O'Connor walked to the window and watched as several men strolled into O'Doyle's Pub across the street from the land office. Suddenly he was thirsty.

"Hurry up, will ya. I'm in dire need of a pint."

Fifteen minutes later the man sprinkled white sand on the document. As it dried the ink on the deed, he opened his log book to the front, turned several pages, and on a line for the purpose, filled in the date, property description, King George V, King of England, grantor, and Jack Paidrig O'Connor, grantee.

"It's official," he said as he handed the deed to O'Connor. "You own your family farm. Let's hope neither of us regrets this day."

O'Connor looked at the deed, carefully folded it once and put it in the portfolio, turned and headed toward the door. He paused with his hand on the door knob and turned back to the man.

"Join me for a pint," he asked, grinning broadly.

-45-

Daichead a cúig

Working the farm was exhilarating and exhausting. Two weeks after moving into his cottage, O'Connor used some of the money from Stratford and his sailor's pay to increase the fine flock of Suffolk sheep that came with the place. He had spent those two weeks cleaning out years of neglect and filth from the house, re-thatching the roof on the house and barn, and repairing the small corral attached to the barn.

On his walk to his own place after getting his deed and drinking a pint with some of the villagers, O'Connor had noticed four occupied farmhouses in some need of repair, so each day he finished his own work before dusk and rode his horse to his furthest neighbor.

The first day he knocked on the front door, yelled to find out if anyone was home. Hearing no answer, he walked around the small front yard and picked up a broken wagon wheel, a rusty baby carriage with one axle missing, and various discarded household items.

Have some pride, O'Connor thought as he threw the trash over the front fence, which he would return to repair in a day or two. At least the front yard was clean now. He would also return with his wagon and collect all the trash he threw close to the road, salvage what he could, and burn the rest.

The story was the same at each house, but the evening he drove his wagon back to the first and furthest house to collect the trash and repair the fence, an elderly woman leaned with both elbows on the fence of the second house and watched him approach.

"Thanks for sprucing up me place," she said. He pulled the reins and the horse stopped and shook his head against the harness.

"You're entirely welcome," he nodded in a small bow. "My name's Jack O'Connor. Who might you be?"

"Maude Leary. Next place on down is my sister Clare. She's not home. Been gone since St. Brigid's Day. Took her husband and child to hospital in Dublin. They got consumption and we don't know how long they got."

O'Connor felt ashamed and embarrassed for what he thought about the people whose place he cleaned up. St. Brigid's Day was months ago.

"Sorry to hear," he mumbled to the woman.

"She'll appreciate coming home to a clean place. When she comes home … If she comes home."

"Then we'll keep it neat and clean until she does," O'Connor said, choking on his words. These softer emotions were new to him, brought on by loving a woman he would never see again. Damn that feckin' British woman.

He climbed down from the wagon and threw the small pile of junk in front of Maude Leary's house into the back of his wagon. "I'll come by the next few days and help you neaten up the whole place," he said to her as he climbed back on the wagon. She smiled and waved as he drove away.

For the next three days O'Connor worked at Clare's cottage, finishing only when he was satisfied with how clean and neat it looked. Like a picture postcard, he thought as he stopped the wagon and looked back at his handiwork.

He visited the place once a week just to maintain its

condition. On the fifth week, he saw smoke rising from the chimney. A two-wheeled cart rested next to the small barn, but there was no horse to be seen. As he got closer, he saw the horse munching on grass in the rear pasture. Not knowing what to do, he wheeled the horse and wagon around in front of the house as quietly as possible. The door burst open and a tall, thin middle-aged woman ran out of the house, yelling at him.

"Stop. Stop, Mr. O'Connor!"

O'Connor drew up the horse and held the reins as he looked down at her. She reached up and grabbed his hand with her bony fingers.

"Thank you, sir, for taking care of our home while we were gone," she sobbed. It did not escape O'Connor that she said 'our' instead of 'my.' Then he saw the tall, rail-thin man standing in the doorway holding a frail-looking boy in his arms. The man was smiling and waving weakly. The boy kept his head on his da's shoulder and his arms and legs wrapped around him. They had survived their illness and had come home to heal and grow stronger in this beautiful place.

"You're a saint," she said through tears of gratitude.

'No, I'm a fighter and a trained killer,' he thought, 'God willing, you'll never see that side of me.'

"No, just trying to be a good neighbor," he replied, the words barely escaping the lump in his throat. She squeezed his hand and let go. "Giddup," he shouted to the horse as he slapped the reins on its back and drove away. 'Damn you, Brigid Andrews. Just damn you!'

And so, without really intending to, Jack O'Connor became the good neighbor to almost everyone in the county. Whenever someone needed his help, that person would mention it to another person who would then approach

O'Connor at the pub or the wool auction.

"Say, Mr. O'Connor, I hear Mrs. O'Toole needs help mending her stone fence. D'ya think you might ever be willing to take a look?" That was how it usually went because people thought it was both rude and embarrassing to ask for help directly. O'Connor knew the game and played along willingly. It gave him a good feeling to help instead of harm.

-46-

Ɗaicheaɗ a sé

Three men walked across O'Connor's pasture. The dog closest to O'Connor spied them first and barked until O'Connor looked toward the men and commanded the dog to hush. At this distance he couldn't recognize their faces, but he could see they wore the refined clothes of city dwellers and they carried shillelaghs.

O'Connor waved. One of the men waved back; the other two kept walking with their heads down to avoid stepping in sheep droppings.

"Mr. O'Connor," hailed the man who had waved.

"Aye," O'Connor answered.

The three men formed a semi circle around O'Connor. The man who had waved, spoke. "I'm Dugan O'Malley, this here's Brian Doyle and Sean Browne," he said pointing in turn at the other two. "Word in town is you own this place free and clear," he said to O'Connor.

"I do."

"Well, not many of us own our places," O'Malley said. "You musta kissed some royal arse," he sneered. Doyle and Browne laughed.

"How can I help ya," O'Connor asked, ignoring the attempted insult.

"Well, now, Mr. O'Connor, we're here to help you help yourself," said O'Malley. "We think a landed gentleman like yourself would want to protect his holdings and would also be a great asset to our cause."

"And what cause would that be," O'Connor asked.

"Irish freedom from the grasp of the Brits," piped up Doyle. He and Browne were now absently hitting their shillelaghs in the palms of their hands.

"Listen, boys, I've had enough fighting for a lifetime. Two lifetimes. I just want to raise my sheep, work my farm, live the quiet life," O'Connor said, and squared off as he looked intently at each of the men, "of a retired British Army guerilla fighter, bare knuckler, and reformed Irish mob assassin."

"We know all about you and how your pa died," O'Malley said, nervously. "Sinn Fein could sure use a man of your many talents."

"Not interested," O'Connor said, glaring at the men, his fists clenched at his sides. "Now please get off me land."

"We'll be back," Doyle said as the three backed away.

"Not if you know what's going to keep you healthy," O'Connor said.

The dogs broke away from the sheep, which were grazing contentedly 50 yards from O'Connor, and ran after the three men, nipping at their heels. Doyle swung his shillelagh at them but they both dodged the blow and danced away, seemingly laughing. They herded the men back to the road, then O'Connor whistled and they ran back to him and sat at either side. He bent down and scratched each dog behind the ears to communicate his approval of what they had done. Master and dogs watched the three men walk down the road until they crested the small hill and disappeared over the top.

O'Connor shook his head and sighed. "I doubt we've seen the last of them," he said to the dogs. And he was right. Anytime he went into town, one of the three Sinn Feiners, usually joined by another man, appeared wherever O'Connor was. Whether he was enjoying a lone pint at O'Doyle's Pub or loading supplies at Finnegan's Mercantile, the radicals watched him.

After a month of their constant spying O'Connor had had enough. He was carrying out a sack of flour from Finnegan's when he saw Dugan O'Malley and a much larger man watching him from their perch in front of the land office. O'Connor's dogs sat on the wagon bench and, recognizing O'Malley, began to growl.

"Stay," O'Connor commanded. The dogs whined, but sat. O'Connor loaded the flour onto the back of the wagon, pulled his trousers higher and walked straight at the men.

"Enough, O'Malley," he said from 20 feet away. "I'll not be joining your band of merry men no matter how much you try to intimidate me into it. I just want to live in peace and enjoy my life. Now, I don't want any trouble from you or your henchman there, but I ain't afraid of a fight and fight him and you I will."

The big man stepped off the Land Office step. He was carrying a large shillelagh in his massive right hand and swung it back and forth at his side as he walked toward O'Connor. He stopped three feet in front of O'Connor and stood with his legs spread wide in what he thought was a perfectly balanced stance to enable him to split O'Connor's skull open with a forceful swing of his club.

'This is far too easy,' O'Connor thought. He looked the larger man straight in the eyes and with his right leg kicked him with all his might right between his spread apart legs. As the man fell forward grimacing in pain and holding his groin with both hands, O'Connor struck him in his Adam's apple with the rigidly folded second knuckles of his right hand. The man struggled for breath and passed out, but still managed to whimper loudly. O'Connor picked up the man's shillelagh, stepped over him and took three steps toward O'Malley, who stared in awe at his fallen enforcer then at the approaching O'Connor.

Thinking better than to engage O'Connor in a fight, O'Malley spread his arms in a gesture of surrender and walked sideways down the Land Office steps and down the street keeping his eyes on O'Connor, who watched him with a bemused look on his face. Before O'Malley was out of sight, O'Connor turned and again stepped over the man as he walked to his wagon and the waiting dogs. As he climbed aboard, several villagers applauded and the ones who had been watching from behind lace curtains smiled at him as he drove away.

O'Connor never saw any of O'Malley or his Sinn Fein gang again, except in the pub, which they promptly and quietly left when he walked in.

-47-

Daichead a seacht

County Cork, Ireland

O'Connor, sat on the small wood and iron plow, guiding his draft horse off the edge of the field where he slid off the plow seat, walked to the hitch and unhitched the horse. O'Connor took up the reins and tied the large horse to a post next to the water trough. As the horse drank, O'Connor removed the harness and threw it over a fence rail. He stroked the horse's neck and withers as he admired his large, freshly plowed field.

When the horse had drunk its fill, O'Connor led it to a stone barn. He backed the horse into a stall, picked up a pitch fork and threw fresh straw into the stall. He kept the barn clean and orderly, but he neatened it up even more as he walked out.

O'Connor walked across his farmyard to the stone cottage, which sported a new thatched roof and freshly whitewashed trim. As he approached the house, something caught his eye, causing him to turn and look up the road leading into the farmyard. A horse and rider approached.

O'Connor took three steps to the corner of his house and tried to make out the person. Recognition washed over his face and he walked to the middle of the road as the horse and rider entered the farmyard.

"Come to finish the job?" he asked the rider.

Brigid Andrews dismounted, dropped the reins and stood squarely in front of O'Connor, hands at her sides, fingers fidgeting with the seams of her riding pants.

"When my father brought a wounded boy into our home all those years ago …," her voice trailed off, tears welling up in her eyes. She walked to him and attempted to put her arms around his neck. O'Connor pushed them away.

"Part of me died when the police hauled you off. But my heart sang when I heard you had gone to Canada," she sobbed.

"You're a snake and a whore," he said derisively. "No, you're worse than a whore. At least a whore is honest."

"Killing you that day on the road just seemed too easy. Then all that time together. I fell in love with you, Jack."

"Attempted murder in a hotel room t'ain't the best way to start a lasting relationship, lass."

"I fell in love, O'Connor, even more when I realized you were that wounded boy."

"You tried to help your Da kill me."

"I went to my father's office to stop him from having you killed. He hired some thugs—Irishmen like you who needed the money. Why do you think he sent Margaret away? They were going to kill you when you left his office building. I saw them, O'Connor. I suppose when the cops drove up they ran away."

"You're lying. Get back on that animal then and leave Ireland, Brit. There's nothing here for you."

"I'll never find my way back to the village in the dark," she lied.

O'Connor looked around in disgust. He brushed past Brigid to her horse and grabbed the reins. Leading the horse past her, he headed to the barn.

"You can sleep in the barn with the other animals. In

the morning, I'll take you back to Armagh. You can catch the first train out."

They walked into the barn, neither of them speaking.

O'Connor unsaddled the horse, hung the tack, and backed the horse in an empty stall. Brigid watched him. "I suppose you expect me to sleep in the stall with that animal."

"I expect you to go to hell. Where you sleep is not my concern, but the horse might object. It needs food and water, though."

O'Connor reached into a large bin, scooped up oats in a feed bag, and put the bag on the horse. He threw hay into the stall.

"When he's done eatin', take off the bag so he can drink from the bucket you're going to bring him."

"Don't go, Jack, I have to tell you something," she said, quietly, then tearfully.

Stunned at her revelation, he turned and walked out of the barn. He closed the barn door and threw down the latch. Brigid walked to the door and looked through a crack to watch him walk to the house. O'Connor opened the door, paused, and looked back into the barn. Brigid, seeing him look back at her, smiled, wiping away her tears. O'Connor snorted and walked to the house, entered, and slammed the door behind him so she wouldn't see him collapse onto the hearth with tears in his eyes.

Brigid settled into a pile of straw in one corner of the barn, pulled a horse blanket over herself, and closed her eyes. Outside, thunder clouds raced past the moon skipping shadows across stone-fenced barley fields and verdant pastures. Lightning cracked flashes at the ground and thunder answered with deafening claps. The darkest clouds flowed violently together and a downpour began to soak the green earth.

The loud thunder startled O'Connor awake, and for the briefest moment, he was huddled in a muddy foxhole listening for the whistle of the Austrian cannon rounds over his head. He sat up and realized that he wasn't covered in mud, and his woolen uniform britches were not water logged. He threw the sheets off and got into the clothes he had hung on a peg by his bed. Earlier, he had sat on the hearth, head in hands, trying to imagine how his life would be different. Finally exhausted and spent from crying, he had shuffled off to bed.

The lightning allowed him to see his way to the front door where he donned a rain slicker and waxed cotton hat. He lit a lamp by the fireplace and then lit a lantern which hung by the front door. Lantern in hand, O'Connor ran across his yard to a pasture beside the house, jumped over the stone fence and raced over the hill to his flock of sheep.

The thunder and sound of the rain hitting the barn's thatched roof troubled the horses. Although they were dry, the claps of thunder scared them. They didn't like what they couldn't see. Their snorting and whinnying fully awakened Brigid, who had been exhausted enough to sleep through the thunder. She heard the storm and went to comfort the horses. She removed each one's feed bag and rubbed their snouts, trying to comfort them in turn. When they had calmed down, Brigid left the stalls and went to the barn door. Peering out through a crack, she saw the light in the house. When she opened the barn door using the rope to lift the outside latch, the wind blew the door open so hard that it knocked her backwards. Rain quickly soaked her pants, but she jumped up and, grabbing the door with both hands, was able to swing it closed and throw down the latch.

The wind drove the rain through Brigid's clothes, and

it felt like it would pierce the skin on her face. She bent into the wind and walked haltingly to the farmhouse. She tried the front door and opened it. She called out to O'Connor, waited, and hearing no response, called out again, louder.

Two border collies raised their heads and growled.

"Shush, now," she said soothingly. The dogs whined and lay back down. At least I can tame these beasts, she thought.

"O'Connor, you awake?"

She waited again and decided that he was either a very heavy sleeper or had gone out to care for some animals somewhere. Drenched and looking like a cat that had fallen into a pond, Brigid wiped the hair from her face and peered around the room. It was cozy, with a low ceiling and dark oak beams, but the walls and ceiling were a brilliant white. Embers glowed in the stone fireplace, so she threw on three logs and watched the flames get higher as they ignited. She picked up the oil lamp, turned up the wick and began to snoop, first looking at the main room. She ran her other hand over the carved beams as she walked to a small window by the door. She noticed that its frame was new, unpainted wood.

Deciding she should gently wake up O'Connor, she held up the lantern at eye level and walked toward the back of the house through a small, narrow hall and into a large bedroom where she saw a large four-poster feather bed that jutted from the center of one wall. The bed's covers had been thrown back.

Brigid slowly looked over the bedroom. It was sparsely decorated, but clean. A large wardrobe sat opposite the bed. In one corner, to her surprise, sat a large copper bathtub, a towel hanging neatly over the side.

Brigid walked out of the bedroom and down the hall to

the small, clean kitchen. She lightly ran her fingers over the pots and copper kettles hanging above the kitchen fireplace.

The chill that settled into her muscles made her shudder, so she placed the lantern on the floor and wrapped her arms around herself. Must get out of these wet clothes, she thought, so she peeled off her wet clothes and, naked, walked to the tub, where she picked up the towel and slowly dried off. As she was rubbing down her legs, she thought she heard bleating. She wrapped the towel around herself and went to her coat, and reached into the pocket.

Hers had been an arduous journey after the trauma of her father's suicide. When Clayton Andrews found out his firm had not gotten the job of designing and overseeing the construction of a new capital building for North Dakota, he had begun drinking heavily, depleting his entire stock of Irish whiskey and French wine, all of which he had brought in from Canada at no small expense.

Sometime between his tenth and fifteenth bottle of Bordeaux, Brigid had come to his house just after sundown to tell him that two days ago his younger brother had fired every architect, draftsman, and secretary, closed the doors to the firm and walked fully clothed into Lake Michigan. His bloated body had just washed up that morning.

Clayton Andrews sat quietly staring at the empty stone fireplace he had even been too drunk to load with logs from the bin next to it. Brigid stood, her shoulders sagging with the weight of what she had just told him. She looked expectantly at him, waiting for a reaction, some words of sorrow.

He guzzled the last of the wine in the glass he was holding and violently threw it into the fireplace.

"You caused this," he yelled at her. "If you had just

killed that focking Mick we would have built that goddamn building!"

"But father, don't you remember," she cried in desperation. "Their telegram said they liked another firm's design far better!"

"Horseshit!" he slurred. "Mine was beautiful. You have ruined everything … my business, my life … you killed your mother … I hate you!"

Stung by his irrational words, Brigid ran out of the house, out the gate, and onto the country road that was just as lonely as her heart. Although her mind told her that laudanum had killed her mother, his damning still crushed her. She was 50 yards away when she heard the gunshot.

She ran. She didn't know how far, but the sun was rising over the lake just as she approached the outskirts of Chicago. The run had helped clear her mind.

The next few weeks had been a blur. The morning after Brigid had given her father the awful news about her uncle, Margaret had discovered Clayton's body slumped in a heap by the fireplace, gun still in his left hand, a crumpled rendering of a building clutched in his right. Devastated as Margaret was by the suicide of her long-time boss and friend, she still had enough loyalty to track down Brigid at the hotel she had moved to after her father had kicked her out of his house. Brigid was too resentful to react because she knew what the gunshot had meant when she heard it as she ran down the gravel road.

She and Margaret had made all the funeral arrangements, buried her father and bought a large, elaborate headstone. The funeral at the First Presbyterian Church of Chicago in Woodlawn was well attended by some of the city's toniest people. At the cemetery, a tall, stout man with a much younger woman at his side, approached Brigid.

"If you don't have plans for your dear father's house," the man said in an upper-crust voice, "I would be willing to pay top dollar, completely furnished, of course."

Apparently not everyone lost their shirts in the crash of '29, Brigid had thought after the house formally changed hands and she deposited the proceeds in one of the city's still solvent banks.

With her mother gone and her father now dead, Brigid decided she had only one option – to go after the man she loved and tell him about the baby they lost when it came far too early.

-48-

Daichead a hocht

O'Connor, dripping wet, chased the last sheep into the barn. He looked over at the straw and the impression Brigid had left. He stooped, picked up a lamb and ran with it cradled in his arms to the house.

Inside, he noticed the lantern was gone, but was casting a narrow beam of light onto the floor in the hall. O'Connor lowered the lamb to the floor and looked around. In a flash of lightning, he noticed the wet footprints on the floor. He reached underneath the rain slicker and pulled out his knife. Hugging the hall wall, he went to the bedroom door, which was slightly ajar. O'Connor used one eye to look through the opening where he saw the lantern on the floor. He pushed the door hard, crouched down and cocked his knife arm back.

Brigid held the hair brush in both hands. The towel was piled at her ankles. "It won't be a fair fight, hair brush against knife."

"You think standing naked in my bedroom is fighting fair?"

"I'm not fighting, Jack."

Brigid approached O'Connor and tentatively placed her naked arms around his neck.

"Not fairly, you're not."

"You didn't travel all this way to tell me about our baby. Why are you really here," he asked.

She sensed his longing, his emotional bond. "Because I love you," she purred, "and I know you still love me."

"Oh, do ya now."

O'Connor grinned and bent down to kiss her. The lamb bleated at them from the hall. Using his right foot, O'Connor pushed the bedroom door closed.

The next morning, as he did every morning, O'Connor arose before dawn to tend to his flock and his other animals. As he quietly dressed he couldn't help but reflect on the woman in his bed. They had made love several times during the night, one waking the other with gentle kissing that quickly turned into passion. How she had found him was somewhat of a mystery to him, but he would ask her later.

"You can't be running away," she said sleepily, "this being your house and all."

"I'll not be running away today, or any time soon," he replied, laughing.

"Can I help?"

"Sleep some more," he said. "I'm just going to see to the animals."

Brigid laid her head back on the pillow and admired his physique. Farm life had been good to him. His hands were strong but gentle, and his shoulders and legs were hard from toiling in the fields and walking behind a plow. It would be a good life with this man, she thought as she drifted back to sleep.

O'Connor walked out into the dim light before dawn. He whistled softly to the dogs. "Some watch dogs you two are," he said to them. They whined and hung their heads at the tone in his voice, so he felt bad about his mild scolding and scratched them both behind their ears. They went out and he gently closed the front door to his cottage so he wouldn't startle the animals or the woman.

The chores he did by rote after weeks of sameness. He loved the smell of fresh hay in the mornings mingled with the aroma of ripening grain and rich dirt. He motioned to his dogs and they herded the sheep through the gate and into the pasture behind the barn. O'Connor followed them, giving quiet commands which the two border collies obeyed immediately.

Another glorious morning, he thought.

One hundred yards to the east, as he had done every morning for the past two weeks, Jake Tilden watched through binoculars as the bucolic scene unfolded before him. He had wanted to pick just the right spot, and so he had observed O'Connor's morning routine from several vantage points in the hills around the farm. He picked his current spot because he could clearly see most of O'Connor's comings and goings.

Tilden was dressed like any other country gentleman. He wore Jodhpur boots, woolen tweed pants, and a heavily starched white cotton shirt under a loden coat – hardly the look that would attract attention.

He put the binoculars down on the grass beside him and opened the long leather case at his side. He grasped the butt of the rifle and pulled out a Sharps. He had cleaned it the night before one more time just to be sure.

Breathing slowly through his nose to minimize the steam breath, he spread out a six-inch square of deerskin on the grass to his left. Then he reached into his coat pocket and pulled out the three cartridges he had loaded especially for this task, laying them neatly on the soft leather. Next, he set up his shooter's tripod and with practiced ease placed the Sharps' barrel in the notch of the tripod.

Satisfied that this was the right spot, the right day, and the right time, Tilden opened the Sharps' chamber, picked up one cartridge, breathed on it, polished the bullet against his coat sleeve, and inserted it. Then he waited. So did the Indian.

The Indian aimed his own Sharps at the white man lying at the top of the hill a hundred yards away. He had followed the man named O'Connor from Toronto, knowing this skinny dog shit eating white man would come to kill O'Connor.

He had tracked them both across North Dakota, Minnesota, and into Chicago. The little man had disappeared, so the Indian followed the big Irishman. It wasn't difficult. The Mick stood out because of his size, and his failed attempts to blend in. The more he tried, the easier it was for the Indian to track him. Tracking O'Connor was like picking out a single Tatanka in the herd, a skill he had mastered as a young hunter to find the animal that would feed the most members of his tribe.

Black Wolf's biggest challenge had been stealth. He had stayed nondescript by dressing like a white man, like a reservation Indian, which he was.

When he was packing to go to Mandan, he told his woman what the skinny white man had been doing to the tribe's young girls.

"I know," she had said. "I wondered when you would once again be a warrior and go after him."

"I know where he lives in Mandan, but if he is gone, I will track him as he tracks another," he told her, "and I will kill him when he thinks he has no troubles."

In Mandan he had just missed the White Devil, and so, an old Lakota, carrying a long leather bag, a large hat box, and a small knapsack, had left his home and traversed the Midwest, hopping trains, staying in missions, all the time following a devil who was unaware that he would die for his sins at the hands of a detested member of the race he considered subhuman.

-49-

Daichead a naoi

Tilden slightly adjusted the sliding sight, and zeroed in on the path he knew O'Connor would take as he walked back to the cottage. He breathed out slowly, held his breath, and gently pulled the trigger just as a woman walked into his sights.

The Lakota aimed his Sharps at a spot just below the other man's neck. At this angle he knew the bullet would enter the head and cause it to burst open. Just as he prepared to shoot, the other man fired a shot and moved to his left to look over the hill at a target below. The Indian pulled his finger off the trigger and watched the devil get to his feet and slink over the ridge.

Tilden's bullet struck Brigid in the back of her right shoulder and tore through her chest three inches above her right breast. She fell hard, bleeding profusely. Deflected by Brigid's rib, the bullet only grazed O'Connor's left side, and he dove to the ground, crawling quickly to Brigid near a stone outcropping above the stream.

"No. No. NO!" O'Connor whispered in her ear as he pressed her shirt tail against the wound. Blood seeped between his fingers. He knew she would die soon if he couldn't staunch the bleeding.

"I won't let you die," he said in her ear. "Not today."

Thinking he'd killed O'Connor, Tilden worked his way down the hill. O'Connor heard him approach. Bleeding from the wound, he kept his hand pressed on Brigid's wound and played dead. When the sound of footsteps told him someone was right next to him, he grabbed and pulled the ankle of whoever was there.

Tilden went down on his hip, but managed to kick out and connect with O'Connor's head. The blow stunned him. In a flash Tilden was up and kicking at O'Connor with the fierceness of a wild horse kicking a wolf.

Stunned by the blows and their quickness, O'Connor struggled to protect himself. Recalling his fight training, he shielded his head with both forearms and caught a kick as it came at his jaw. Grabbing the foot and twisting, he threw the other man down and lurched to his feet.

But the little man was wiry and drove his shoulder into O'Connor's injured side. The blow knocked O'Connor against the rocks, stunning him momentarily. Seeing an opening, Tilden drew out a Bowie knife and raised his hand to drive the large blade into O'Connor's chest. Just as his arm started its downward motion, Tilden felt a sharp pinch in his back, which immediately became a searing pain in his chest as the bullet exploded from his body. As he fell to the ground, Tilden heard the distinctive report of the old Indian's Sharps rifle, the last sound he would ever hear.

When he saw blood burst from the Evil One's chest and saw him slump over, the Indian slowly placed the Sharps in the case and gathered his things. He walked down the hill toward the road. When he got on the road, he stopped and smiled. It had been a good kill.

"My granddaughter will sleep in peace," he said out loud to the sky. Then, still smiling, he set down the hat box and reached in. He placed the war bonnet on his head because white men thought that's what all Indians wore all the time.

He could convince these Irish that he was off to join a Wild West Show. They would believe him because they wanted to believe in wild Indians.

Ignoring the searing pain in his side, O'Connor crawled on hands and knees to boulders in the stream, collected moss, crawled back to Brigid, and pushed it against her exit wound. He got to his feet and put his arms under her knees and shoulders. It was then that he felt the blood oozing from her back. Moaning at the discovery, he pushed his hand against the hole and stumbled to the house.

The dogs barked wildly as O'Connor kicked open the cottage door. He rushed through the hall and laid Brigid on the bed, removed her boots and clothes, and examined the wounds. The bullet had missed Brigid's vital organs, but the blood loss was nearly fatal. O'Connor had stopped the bleeding front and back, but she drifted in and out of consciousness. Working feverishly with a curved tack-repair needle that he soaked in whiskey, he first sewed up her gaping chest wound. She never cried out or even moaned as he stitched her up with thick black thread.

Rolling her over he saw the bedding was soaked in blood, but the hole was merely oozing. He quickly stitched up the smaller wound and gently rolled her back over. Her face was so pale that he feared she might die right then, so to get blood back to her head, he propped up her feet with a pillow.

It was only when she was stable that he again felt the pain in his side. O'Connor took a long pull on the whiskey and using the same needle and thick thread, stitched up his wound.

During the day, he was like an expectant father pacing outside the birthing room. Every few minutes he would check on Brigid to see if she was still alive. At night he slept fitfully on the floor next to the bed, waking often to look at the rise and fall of her chest.

On more than one occasion during the first days after being shot, she briefly stopped breathing. Using his best battlefield first aid, O'Connor had gently pushed in the middle of her chest until she breathed on her own.

On the fourth day, Brigid woke up while O'Connor was burying Tilden. When he came in, he immediately went to the bedroom to check on her. As he walked through the bedroom door, she looked at him and through cracked lips, said, "Can't a girl get a drink around here?"

~50~

CAOGA

Jack O'Connor stood at the crest of a lush green hill overlooking his farm. As he surveyed the scene below, he smiled. His two horses roamed the corral next to the barn. A few meters from the barn, his stone-fenced fields stood tall with ripening oats and barley. His large flock of Suffolks grazed contentedly in a pasture where the body was buried in an unmarked grave overgrown with grass. O'Connor's two Border Collies rested nearby enjoying the sun on their backs. Feeling contented beyond his own belief, he walked down to the barn and thought about how his life had changed.

In the two years since the incident, Brigid and Jack had tended to each other's wounds and the farm. Under O'Connor's sometimes impatient guidance, she had proven a quick study about the sheep and the land. Once they recovered from their wounds, they worked the farm together sharing all the chores, most often together. They had reminisced for hours about the details of O'Connor's stay at her father's estate. They argued about how the British government treated the Irish, he always siding with the impoverished Irish, she trying in vain to justify British government policy.

After their fourth or fifth heated discussion, they both stopped talking and began to laugh at the insanity of arguing about the past. From then on, their only argument, which was never really an argument, was how often they would make love.

He was in the barn repairing the yoke on his wool wagon when he heard her voice.

"Jack, the priest is here.

Brigid approached, a redheaded year-old baby straddled her hip.

"What's the old bastard want?"

"He says he'll baptize Marlene this Sunday after Mass under one condition."

"And what would that be?"

"That he marries us first."

O'Connor laughed and took Marlene from Brigid. The baby giggled as he swung her around high in the air. Handing her back to Brigid, he took her hand and walked out of the barn. He looked out over his fields and marveled about the life he never thought he would have. Smiling, he turned to face the two most important people in his life and slowly got down on one knee and took Brigid's hand.

"Well, then, will ya marry me, Darlin'?"

– An Deireadh –

About the Author

Patrick James Brown is a professional writer who has written for publication since high school. He is the author of an award-winning one act play, numerous magazine articles, a non-fiction account of North Dakota's statehood centennial celebration, a plethora of successful advertising and public relations campaigns, and a children's book. The Mick is his first novel. He grew up in Bismarck, North Dakota and currently lives in Fargo, North Dakota.

Author photo by Mark Anthony, Visionaries Photography.